AVA

Alexander Dumsein

Contents

Ava and her loved ones took a trip to the Golden State two summers ago. Ava's summer with the charming Max was a highlight of her life. The chemistry between them was electric. Ava felt as though she were in a dream. Possibly because Max destroyed her heart by cheating on her the day before they were both ready to go their separate ways. There was a time when she believed he loved her and would make an effort to stay in touch.

Ava fled California after her heartbreak and found a new person when she returned. Two years later, upon relocating to Los Angeles, Ava once again crosses paths with Max.

Ava's life feels like it's out of her control as her heart continues to heal and the very attractive Max wants to apologise, explain himself, and try to win her back.

Including her crush on the bad boy at her new school, Ava has a lot to deal with.

1

1 | Where It All Started

"Max stop!" I shriek as he hoists me into the air like I weigh nothing. I giggle as he starts to spin me around on the beach.

"Nah, I'm not finished with you yet." I could hear the smile in his voice as he continued to spin me around. People around me were staring at us or giving us looks of adoration. It made me feel a bit embarrassed that we were showing some PDA.

If my back wasn't facing Max's chest, I would have sent him a nasty glare.

Eventually, Max put me down on the sandy beach. And me being the childish 16-year old that I am, bent over and picked up a handful of sand and threw it at Max. What I didn't seem to consider was that sand isn't snow. The sand didn't stick together so majority of the bits ended up missing Max.

"Well, that didn't—"

"Shut up." I cut Max off.

"Sure thing sunshine." Max teases, using the pet name I hated. Since I met him a couple of months ago, all Max would do was tease me with the nickname I hate: sunshine. To say it irritated me was an understatement.

We were both on holiday and we were staying at the same hotel. We met after I spilled my ice cream all over Max's white top at the hotel pool. I had expected him to shout at me but instead, he laughed and said I should probably get a new ice cream.

After apologizing and offering to buy him an ice cream too, we started talking. And from there we hit it off.

I've spent the majority of my holiday with Max. We've spent most of the time at the beach or at the water park. We even started dating, which amazes me. Max was super hot, like crazy hot whilst I'm ordinary.

I know I shouldn't care but a part of me feels insecure. I feel like he'll dump me for another girl, one who is prettier and better than me. I guess I'm as afraid as every other girl.

"Do you wanna head back?" Max asks as he runs a hand through his silky brown hair. It looks puffy and soft. I just love running my hand through his hair.

"Sure." I agree, smiling as he stretches his large hand out to me. My smaller hand fits his perfectly, like two pieces of a jigsaw puzzle.

We start walking along, me smiling at the passers-by. I could see the hotel as we neared it, the glamorous really stood out. It has a long driveway that was surrounded by palm trees, with a fountain at the end where the grand doors were.

In the lobby, they have a bar, a waiting area, the lifts and of course, the reception desk. The hotel has many floors, each having a balcony that overlooked the stunning beach. My room was one below from Max's, so we could communicate whenever.

"Hi, Jeff." I give a big smile at the doorman, who I have taken a liking to. He reminds me of my late Grandfather, who was always kind to others, no matter how bad he was feeling.

"Miss O'Connor. Did you have a nice stroll?" Jeff asks, a knowing smile on in his face that had me blushing like a tomato.

"Oh, you can bet we did," Max smirks, the jerk enjoying my embarrassment. I give Max a playful glare as I stick my tongue out at Jeff. Max rolls his eyes at my childish behavior. "Wow, aren't you mature."

I grin back at him. "Oh, you can bet I am."

Max tries not to smirk at me copying his words but fails.

Max leads me through the lobby and up to my room. It is a thing we did after a day out. We'd choose a movie to watch and cuddle up on the bed.

"So what are we watching today?" Max casually asks as he falls onto my bed.

I ponder on what to watch. "Hmm, I dunno. Let me look on Netflix."

Max hands me my remote that was on the table beside my bed and lets me flick through some movies. I am fancying a romance, partly to get back at Max for what he did earlier. Spinning me in the air like a rag doll is not how you treat a lady.

Eventually, I find one of my favorite films. As soon as Max sees what I chose, he groans.

"There is no way you are making me watch that."

"Of course I'm going to make you watch that. Its an important, iconic film. You have to watch it." I tell him, pressing play.

Immediately, the film went to the beautiful house by the lake. I have always loved how magnificent it looked; on a number of occasions, I have thought about Googling where the house was—just so I could visit it.

After 10 minutes, Ryan Gosling's younger face came onto the screen. If you were guessing that we were watching The Notebook, then you got the right answer.

Every time I watch this amazing film, I cry. Unfortunately, I'm a sucker for romances like this. I'm like every other teenage girl who wished they had a man like Noah. A man who was devoted to me, who put me first, who loved me was my dream.

2 hours later

I sniffle as I wipe my face with my arm sleeve. Once again, I had a break down at how romantic it was. I glance at Max to see his light brown eyes trained on the screen. He is staring at it with such intensity, he just had to be deep in thought.

I decide not to be nosy and ask him, instead I just let him continue. Perhaps he felt a bit upset and his man pride wouldn't allow him to cry. Once my tears have settled down, I bring Max back to reality.

"So..." I start. "Want to watch something else?"

Max doesn't reply at first so me being the nice person I am, I push him off of the bed. That should wake him up.

"Hey!" Max protests, getting up. "Was that necessary?"

I nod my head, a small smile on my face as he adorably pouts. Yes, pouts. A grown sixteen-year-old who looked like an Adonis model pouted like a five—year—old. It is comical.

"What do you want to do now Max?"

Max runs a hand through his hair as stands up. "I don't know sunshine. I think I might have an early night, you know, start some packing now?"

Now it was my turn to pout, upset that he is ditching me. "But—"

"Ava, I promise I'll make it up to you tomorrow. We can spend the whole day together. Its just otherwise I won't have time tomorrow to pack."

Max is being logical. We are leaving in two days, going to different states. We should probably pack for it now so that I could spend the whole of tomorrow with him.

And plus, we are going to be staying in contact, chatting online. And we discussed meeting up on weekends and weeks off when we have a holiday. So we would still see and hear from each other.

"Okay." I sigh in defeat, sagging my shoulders.

"See you tomorrow beautiful," Max says and kisses my forehead. I close my eyes, savoring the moment. The contact ignited electricity, that had my stomach turning upside down.

It was magical.

Max walked out of the door with a final wave. I lied down on my bed and stared at the ceiling. I guess packing some items now would be a good idea.

***

The next day, I wake to the sun shining brightly on my face. I felt refreshed showering last night.

Yawning, I step out of my bed and walk over to my balcony. The sky is completely blue and the sun is shining brightly. Some dog walkers are walking along the beach and some surfers are tackling the waves.

To wake up here every day, with such a beautiful sight would be a dream.

I hear a girl's giggle somewhere close by. I frown, confused as I can't see anyone above me. Just when I thought I imagined it, I hear it again but louder. It is coming from down below.

Looking over the railing's to where Max's balcony was, I see something that would stay embedded in my brain forever. A drop dead gorgeous girl with blonde hair and blue eyes stands on his balcony, wearing one of Max's favorite tops. Max is opposite her, his chest bare as he smiles at the girl. His hair is ruffled and he looks happy. It doesn't take a genius to work out what they had done.

My heart breaks as I realize he cheated on me, with a girl who is so stunning. That's why he wanted to leave early yesterday, not to pack but to hook up with a girl.

I cover my mouth with my hand, trying to stifle a sob as I run back into my room.

How could he do that to me?!

I quickly run around my room packing everything, not bothering to tidy my clothes. I can feel some tears fall down my cheeks. I don't want to cry. I want to be strong but the first guy I ever loved just cheated on me, dumped me for somebody better. My insecurities were right.

Max didn't want to be with me. He probably just wanted to use me. He probably wanted to see if I was an easy lay.

I bite my lip to stop myself from sobbing, nearly drawing blood.

No. You are not going to cry.

Once I finish packing, I take the last piece of paper on the desk and the pen and write a letter.

A letter to him.

***

Placing the letter outside of his door, I walk to my parents to tell them I want to go home a day early. I just can't tell them why because they like Max's parents and I don't want to ruin their friendship just because Max was a dick.

After talking to them, they agree that its okay for me to leave. I wave them a goodbye as I board the plane. I am so thankful to go home where I can do the traditional girl thing and cry whilst binge-watching Netflix shows.

I vow to myself that I am never going to make the same mistake again and trust a guy. Especially one like Max.

I hate him.

I despise him for now ruining my outlook on life. I swear, if I ever see him again I am going to make him pay for breaking my heart.

Now, because of him, my heart would never be the same.

Little did I know my heart is going to turn cold. Little did I know it is going to build wall after wall to protect itself.

I am never going to fall for a man again. That is a promise.

2

2 | The Move

2 years later

I groan as I finish packing the final box. Everything is done, everything is packed.

I can't believe we are actually doing this, moving to somewhere new. I love my life here, I love the friends I have. Moving away means leaving everything behind, something that I hate.

"Ava, are you done?" My mom shouts from downstairs.

"Yeah," I shout back and lift the lightest box up.

Mom and dad are both taking stuff to the moving truck when I finally made it downstairs. I give the box to one of the men whilst I look around my living room for one last time. It is empty, everything ready to be taken.

The mantlepiece doesn't have any of the photos my parents have taken of me, the TV and the table are gone, the ornaments around the room gone as well. It makes me sad, seeing my home like this.

"Come on sweetie." My mom says, taking my hand. "You'll like the new home, I promise."

"Sure," I mutter under my breath as she drags me to our car. As soon as I am seated, I plug my headphones in. The best way to drown my sorrows is by listening to my favorite music.

My dad gets into the driver's seat and starts the car. I look at my house for the last time, capturing the last moment of it.

The lawn is neat with the flowers growing, a sold sign was pitched on the grass. The actual house looks new and ready to be loved again. Just not by me this time.

I sigh as I begin my journey to my new life, already missing my old life.

6 hours later

I hate traffic. No, I despise it.

Of course, we get stuck in traffic after a major accident. I honestly don't think luck is on my side right now. We had to wait at least two hours to get out of the chaos and let me tell you, it was a nightmare.

I'm not the only impatient person in my family, my dad is just as bad as me. He spent the majority of the time cursing at the cars in front of us and then blamed the GPs for making us go onto that particular highway.

"Well, would you look at how beautiful the house is?" My mum cheerfully says as we stop at our new house. When I say house, I mean mansion. I honestly don't know why they bought a house that looked like it was built for about ten people.

"Sure." I agree, opening the car door and stretching my limbs. I went through several moments of pins and needles due to sitting down for too long.

The mansion—I mean house—had a color theme of white, with all of the bricks being white, the doors painted white etc. The garden is pretty though, perfectly lawned, with flowers sections in the middle and in front of the house.

There are three steps that lead to the double doors, with two statues standing at the front. If you ask me, it looks like we are walking into a celebrity home.

Inside the house, there is a staircase, with the living room to the right and the kitchen to the left. The dining room is behind the kitchen and the laundry room was situated after the corridor that passed the basement door and the dining room. The rooms are all massive, way too big for three people.

"Why don't you go and choose the best room sweetie? I believe there are four to choose from, excluding our room." My mom sweetly asks as she takes her sunglasses off.

I nod my head and head up the staircase. The house smells like lavenders, which I find odd. Why would someone try and make the house smell of lavenders?

On the landing, there is a mini table that would be filled with one of my mom's precious ornaments. There are two corridors going in opposite directions. One way leads to three rooms, one being my parent's room which has an en-suite. Another being the spare bathroom and a study room.

I start walking the other way, passing the extra cupboard that would be filled with blankets. The walls are painted a beige color and some paintings of natural places hung where there was room.

The first room I pas doesn't really take to my liking. It is a tiny room that would be used either as a guest room or my library. The second room is a bit bigger but I still don't like it. It is a rectangular room that has a walk-in wardrobe, a desk, and a double bed. That would be the main guest bedroom.

The last room is my favorite. It is going to be my room.

It has a double bed with two windows situated on either side, both leading to a balcony that looks out over the massive garden that has a pool. There is a walk in wardrobe to the left that has room for a shoe section, a dress section, and a normal clothes section. It also has a mini desk inside that would be used for my jewelry.

On the right, there is an en—suite, with a bath, shower and a tap with a mirror. It looks modern and just plain fancy.

To the left of the door when you enter, is a massive desk that has a notice board over the wall. Draws are also put against a wall for some of my photos.

Overall, I fall in love with the room.

I fall onto the bed and sigh. Perhaps I could grow to like this room. I mean, once I set everything up and put all of my books in my library, it would feel better. After all, home is where you make it, not where you come from.

"Ava, do you want to take some of the light boxes up to your room?" My dad asks as he steps into my room carrying a heavy box. His eyes exam the room and flashes with approval. "Nice choice kiddo."

"Dad," I whine. "I'm not a kid anymore. I'm 18."

"But you'll always be my baby girl."

I playfully roll my eyes, a small smile forming on my face that I try to hide.

"Your mother is making me put all of her stuff away, she's complaining that she has to observe it being put there to make sure its okay." My dad says.

"Sounds like mom," I reply, knowing too well what my mom is like.

"Well." My dad starts. "Have fun, dinner should be done around nine." I nodded my head and opened the box my dad brought up.

Might as well start here.

It takes longer then I thought. But it is worth it because my room looked pretty neat. Better than my previous room. I check the time and see I have half an hour until dinner so I decided to catch up on some Netflix. More specifically, The Vampire Diaries.

I have been obsessed with the Salvatore brothers for ages, they are just so hot. What I would do for a guy like that...

Anyways, I put on another episode and relished in the hotness. What? You can't judge a girl for well, being a girl.

"Ava!" My mom shouts from downstairs thirty minutes later. I pause the episode and get off of my bed. As I rush down the stairs and stumble into the dining room where I can smell the food. And boy, did it smell good.

My mom has always been an amazing cook. I wish I had inherited her cooking skills but unfortunately, I hadn't. Me and my dad can't cook to save our lives. We discovered this when we tried to make a meal for my mom on her birthday. Let's just say it didn't end well, mostly because we had to make a 911 call.

Yeah...lets just not relive that moment.

"Smells good mom." I compliment her as I sit down in our new dining room.

"Thanks, honey." My mom gives me a warm smile and dishes out some of the food.

The meal was delicious. I enjoyed every second. In fact, I nearly had an orgasm from its perfection. Extreme but true.

"So tomorrow you'll have some free time but after that, you'll be enrolling in school." My dad informs me, putting his knife and fork on his plate.

I mentally groan, wanting to die. Starting at a new school was going to be dreadful.

"Do I have to?" I asked him, giving him my puppy eyes.

"Yes," I open my mouth to refuse. "No more discussions on it." Closing my mouth, I slump in my seat as my dad gets up to take the plates out.

My mom stays and gives me a soft smile. "It won't be that bad, you'll fit in." And with that, she gets up to help my dad with the dishes.

"That's what you think," I mutter aloud to no one.

Moving here was not a good idea.

3

3 | Sorry Guys, You Just Aren't My Type

Westmount high is crowded. The halls are packed with teenagers who are all excited to see each other after a summer away. I can barely move without getting barged into.

The people here are rude and inconsiderate. Not one of them apologized for pushing me into a locker or making me almost drop my stuff. I had to hold my tongue from biting back at them.

I want to make a good first impression and that meant not being known as the girl who doesn't take shit from anybody. After all, first impressions are very important.

I try to bypass the students, sometimes hitting their shoulders. Why was everything here so awkward?

"Excuse me," I mumble, pushing through a group who are stood outside of the reception office. Two of the girls, whose faces were caked in make—up and are wearing clothes that would fit my ten—year—old cousin, glare at me.

Ignoring them, I walk into the open office and breathe. The office is nice and spacious; not many students are in here. I can barely hear everyone outside, which I am counting as a good thing.

I approach the desk where a lady with grey hair is typing. She looks tired and defeated. Overall, she looks like she doesn't want to be here. Same here.

"Hi." I politely greet, standing in front of the desk. Her brown eyes look up and she gives me a small smile.

"Hello, honey. Are you new?" She asks and I nod. "Well, welcome to Westmount High. Can I take your name please?"

I nod and tell her my name. My fingers tap on the desk as I wait for her to print out my timetable and give me all of the necessary details.

Eventually, she finishes and hands me the sheet. "Here you are sweetie. I'll get someone to show you around the school."

I open my mouth to tell her that I don't need anyone, that I can find my own way around but she beats me, by clicking the speaker and calling out a 'Molly Holland'.

Quicker then what I expect, a black haired girl comes up to me. She's around 5"5 and has long, silky black hair that I'm immediately envious of. Her chocolate brown eyes are small, maybe a bit too small for her face but with her soft features, it makes her look cute.

"Hi, I'm Molly." She beams, holding out her hand. She looks like one of those people who is always happy, bright and welcoming.

She reminds me of myself from two years ago.

"Hello, I'm Ava." I smile, taking her hand and shaking it. Her hand is small and tanned, like the rest of her. Her tanned complexion makes her look absolutely stunning, I've always wanted olive colored skin. The way it contrasts with her pitch black hair makes me envious of her, again.

"Great!" She says excitedly. "Let me show you around. And if you'd like, we could sit together at lunch."

Wow, she's really nice. I have already put myself in the loner mindset today, knowing I wouldn't make any friends today.

"That's really kind of you," I say, opening the doors to the packed hallways.

Molly surprises me by linking her arm with mine; leads me down the hallways. I notice she's holding my timetable and is muttering to herself 209, my locker number to myself. Most people would think she's strange, muttering to herself but I find it quite amusing. I myself, mutter to myself.

I observe her, how her body language looks closed. When I first met her, she seemed like an open person who was an extrovert but perhaps I was wrong. Maybe she's only open to people she's comfortable with. It makes me happy that she feels comfortable around me.

"What?" Molly asks, raising her head to look at me, her eyes curious. Dammit, now she might think I'm acting like a creep.

"Nothing." I shake my head, a small smile on my face.

"Tell me." She pouts, her light pink lips jutting out. Her eyes are pleading with mine to answer her.

I sigh, running a hand through my hair. "I thought I was the only weird person who talked to their self."

She laughs, her eyes gleaming with something.

"I know right! Everyone says I'm crazy."

I nod my head in agreement. "Yeah, that amount of times people have said I should be checked out by a psychiatrist is unreal."

We both burst into giggles. I feel like we're bonding. The way we talk to each other is like we're old friends, not two strangers who just met each other. I can tell that we are going to be good friends, maybe even best friends.

***

She shows me around the school and takes me to my locker. All the while, we talk about ourselves, including what we like and hate etc.

I found out that Molly has a brother who is a couple of months older than her. She says he's a football player and is popular. She lives with both of her parents, her brother: Josh and her cat: Fluffy.

Molly likes listening to Taylor Swift (who I don't mind, some of her songs are good). She likes to draw—she said she wants to become an artist. Molly also said she loves watching things on Netflix, like me. She watches Stranger Things, The Vampire Diaries and a bunch of films.

We are so similar yet so different. She likes to read and stay at home; I like too, at times. After everything that happened two years ago, I changed. I love to party and make out with guys but I also like to read, hang out with friends and watch films.

I don't count myself as a slut, I just like to make out with guys. I love the attention, like any other girl. Plus I learned the hard way that guys only want you for sex.

"Molly, I feel like your my long lost sister," I claim, shutting my new locker shut.

Molly laughs at me and agrees.

"What do you have first?" I ask her, checking my timetable as well to see I have History. Great, my favorite subject.

"History with Mr. Bryan." She answers, her shoulders slouching.

I squeal with excitement and she looks at me in confusion. "We have the lesson together."

She cheers with me and links arms with me.

We walk down the halls and I now begin to notice how a lot of people's attention are on me. They must be curious, after all, I am the new girl. We all know that when someone new arrives, everybody has to know everything about them.

A lot of the boys are checking me out. Maybe wearing skinny jeans and a crop top that just goes past my belly button wasn't a good idea.

We pass a group of good-looking guys who were not so discreetly eyeballing me.

"Molly!" A guy with black hair shouts. Molly turns to look at him and gives him a small smile. I look at the two of them in confusion until I properly see the similarities between them. Both of them have pitch black hair, tanned skin, and chocolate brown eyes. That has to be Josh, her older brother.

He beckons us to come over and begrudgingly, I do.

"Hi, are you new because I've never seen a girl as gorgeous as you here before." A guy with brown hair flirts with me causing me to roll my eyes.

"Yeah, I am," I tell him. "And no, I'm not going to get with you. You don't look my type."

Some of the guys snicker at his disappointed face. Molly gives me a questioning look and I just shrug.

"Well, aren't you feisty?" Josh says, his eyes trailing down my body. "And sexy."

I purse my lips together. "Look, buddy, I won't be getting with you either. In fact, I won't be getting with any of you."

They all look depressed at my words, not that I care though. Molly smirks at me.

"Okay then. Can we at least know your name?" Another boy asks. He has white hair and blue eyes. I hate to admit it but he looks quite attractive, with his hard features and good build. Honestly, they all look attractive. They must be part of the popular group.

"Ava."

They nod their heads and I wait for them to tell me theirs.

When they don't tell me their names, I can tell there must have been some miscommunication. "Your turn."

Quickly, they all step in to tell me their names. Josh introduces himself first, then the brown haired guy who tried to get with me first. Turns out his name is Luke.

Then the white-haired guy who I find very attractive. His name is Lawrence. A nice name for a pretty guy.

The last one to introduce himself looks more apprehensive. I give him a reassuring smile and he seems to feel a bit more comfortable. Like Molly, he looks shyer towards new people.

"Harry."

"Nice to meet you guys. I'm guessing you're all athletes?" They nod their head and I continue. "Football?"

Once again, they nod their heads and I smile in triumphant. I'm great at guessing.

"Sorry, quick question that I have to ask." Luke butts in, looking at me. "How the hell are you so pretty?"

I feel a bit caught off guard by his question. He said it like he's never seen anyone pretty before. I know I'm not ugly but I'm not that pretty. I bet there are people here who are super gorgeous, like model gorgeous.

"Uh...I'm not that pretty," I say and before Luke can protest, Josh jumps in. I feel quite thankful so I send him an appreciative smile. I don't really like people saying something that I'm not, it brings my hopes up.

"So Ava, where are you from?" Josh curiously asks me, mouthing a 'no problem' to me after. The others all look interested, including Molly. I forgot I hadn't told her yet.

"Well, I moved from Cali but I was born in London," I tell them. Molly looks a bit shocked at the London part.

"Really? London, that's so cool. I thought I could hear a British accent." She claims, smiling at me.

Yeah, I still have my British accent, which people find attractive. Not sure why. I hate it.

I am happy I didn't lose it though, it reminds me of my grandparents who live there. We only visit them once a year because it takes so long to get there.

"What's California like?" Lawrence asks me; before I can answer him, Luke and Harry also fire questions at me.

"Why did you move?"

"Are you staying here for long?"

Before I can answer their questions, the bell goes off.

"Well, I guess we'll see the both of you at lunch," Luke says, waving goodbye to us.

Me and Molly also walk off to calculus, my mind slightly dampening. I'm happy that I made some more friends who seem accepting.

Maybe moving here was a good idea.

I'm happy I didn't lose it, it reminds me of my grand-parents who live there. We only visit them once a year because it takes so long to get there.

"What's California like?" Lawrence asks me; before I can answer him, Luke and Harry also fire questions at me.

"Why did you move?"

"Are you staying here for long?"

Before I can answer their questions, the bell goes off.

"Well, I guess we'll see the both of you at lunch," Luke says, waving goodbye to us.

Molly and I also walk off to calculus, my mind slightly dampening. I'm happy that I made some more friends who seem accepting.

Maybe moving here was a good idea.

4

4 | Bumping Into The Devil

The first few lessons were dreadful. The teachers decided to torture me, even though they didn't even know me, by making me introduce myself in front of the class. I had to tell everyone my name, where I came from and why I'm here.

I kind of felt sorry for the people who were in the same classes as me, they had to hear me repeat it.

By now, it is lunchtime and I have never been so glad to eat food. Food is my life, I just can't live without it. Like everyone else.

"Come on Ava, I want to get there soon otherwise we'll get the rubbish food." Molly whines, dragging me along quicker. I thought all school food was rubbish? Is she suggesting that the food here might actually be nice?

At my old school, the lunch food was dreadful. Practically nobody ate it, except for the people who forgot their packed lunch. I honestly have no idea what they put in the food but let me tell you, it was the most disgusting thing I had ever had. It put greasy chips to shame.

"I'm trying," I say, my arm slightly hurting from her pull. Who knew she had such strength? I swear she's stronger then me and I'm bigger than her!

Eventually, we make it into the cafeteria. I breathe a sigh of relief once Molly lets go of my arm and start rubbing it.

I follow her to the short lunch line, whilst observing the cafeteria. I assume this school is a cliche school, where the clique groups sit at certain tables but boy I'm wrong. Everyone sits with anyone, it's mixed, from the cheerleaders to the geeks. There wasn't a single table for a certain group of people, or at least, that's what I saw.

I'm guessing they have a popular group who sit at the popular table because let's face it, every school has that group.

I'm also curious to know if they have the bitchy cheerleaders, with a ruthless Queen B who loves to inflict pain on others.

"What would you like miss?" A dinner lady asks me, her face looking depressed. Her voice is monotone but cold. The stare she is giving me sent shivers down my spine.

Creepy.

"Uh...I'll have the pizza," I tell her, keeping my eyes on my tray. If I look into her soulless eyes any longer, she might take me to hell with her.

She dumps my pizza on my plate and I rush over to Molly who is paying for her food.

Note to self: don't buy food from here anymore.

"Let's go!" Molly chirps as I finish paying.

Molly leads us to the table that Josh and everyone else is sat at. I can't help but smile at that, I could see them being my new friends here. It made me happy that they accepted me so quickly as well.

"Ava! It's so good to see you." Luke smirks, whilst I roll my eyes at him. Please don't tell me he's going to try to flirt with me again.

I ignore Luke and start to eat my pizza. It doesn't taste that bad, it's better than the one back at my old school but then again, that really isn't saying much.

"So, how were lessons?" Lawrence asks me, his white hair falling over one of his eyes. He's got this mysterious aura around him that intrigues me. I know I said I wouldn't date any of these guys but I didn't say anything about looking at them. Lawrence is very attractive, his white hair is unique and new. I definitely feel attracted to him.

"Awful. Why are teachers so cruel?" I rhetorically ask them. Do they really take satisfaction in humiliating and torturing us students? Are there lives really that sad?

"What do you have next?" Josh curiously asks me.

"P.E." I sigh.

I hate sports. I can play it, to a certain degree but when it comes to running or dodgeball, I'm out. Every time I play any sport that has a ball, I always end up injured. I don't know why balls hate me, I have never done anything mean to them.

One time, I was playing at my old school with my best friend, Rosie. I was doing everything I was supposed to, dodging incoming balls and trying to throw them at the other team yet I ended up getting knocked out.

I remember waking up in the infirmary, with a bruised head and a horrible headache. After that, my teacher gave me a free pass for the game.

"Oh dear." Molly gives me a sympathetic look.

"I'm going to die," I exclaim.

"Nah, you'll be fine. I'll save you." Luke flirts, winking at me.

I glare at him. Did he blank out the part where I said I wouldn't date him? "That's okay Luke, I'm perfectly capable of looking after myself."

"But—"

I cut him off with a stone cold glare. How do I try and get him to read the message that I don't need help?

"Mate, I would give up. Ava clearly isn't interested in you. Why don't you go and find some cheerleader or something?" Lawrence whispers to Luke, loud enough for me to hear.

Thank you, Lawrence, maybe advice from a friend will get it into his head.

"But all of the cheerleaders are plain compared to her," Luke whines back quietly. I don't really know if I should be grateful that he finds me that attractive. I mean, its definitely going to boost my confidence. But...I don't want to date him.

Lawrence rolls his eyes, giving up.

"Oh god, here comes queen bitcheria." Molly groans, her lip curling upwards in disgust.

I look over my shoulder to see a young blonde haired girl, who has a lot of make-up on her face and clothes that are too short on. Following her, are two other girls who look like exact copies of her.

They all sneer at people who try to approach them, their eyes showing disgust. Like the people are below them, not as good as them.

I already hate them.

"Let me guess, the stereotypical sluts who 'rule' this school," I whisper to the group and they all nod their heads.

"Great," I mutter sarcastically, watching the three girls go and sit with a group of jocks. Well, when I say sitting, I mean sitting on their laps. The leader of the group immediately starts to suck the face off of one of them.

I look away in disgust. I mean, she could at least have some class.

"That's her boyfriend," Molly states, pointing her head at them. "The captain of the football team."

I expected that. Stereotypical Queen B with the stereotypical captain of the football team.

"I'm guessing they're the popular group," I ask and once again, they nod.

"Not all of them are there though. Max seems to be missing." Josh says, looking around.

My heart slightly constricts at 'Max'. Every time I hear that name, my heart goes weird whilst rage boils in me. It can't be the same Max so I don't need to be angry but I am.

I hate him. So much. He ruined me, made me a different person. Because of him, I'm somebody I don't want to be, somebody insecure who makes out with guys at parties, who doesn't find herself pretty.

He made me her and I will forever hate him for it.

I need to stop thinking about him, it's not like I will ever see him again.

"Who's Max?" I curiously ask, swallowing at the name. Nobody seems to notice my discomfort though or if they did, they don't point it out.

"The 'bad boy' of the school," Molly informs me. "Well, he is now. 2 years ago he wasn't but after a trip somewhere, he became one. It's kind of weird though."

Molly frowns whilst I look at her to continue. The boys are all in their own discussions now so they can't fill in for Molly.

"He doesn't date at all, doesn't even look at girls. I think he went on holiday and something happened to him. He completely changed into someone different. He's scary, like really scary. The boys talk to him at times and say there's a spark missing in his eyes. Like he's there but not really." Molly explains.

"Huh. What do you think happened?" I ask her, leaning in.

"Me, personally? I think he met a girl, fell in love and then lost her. He was so nice before that summer but then afterward, he became cold and distant. He doesn't even go near girls, he acts like their the plague. I know Alessandria, the Queen B tried to get with him but he wouldn't allow him. He looked like it pained him too. I think he's still in love with that girl and he can't let her go. The look in his eyes, it's scary. He looks dead. Whoever he fell in love with, meant a lot to him." Molly finishes, looking slightly sad.

Poor guy. I kind of know what he's going through except for the fact that I'm not pining for her/ him.

"Oh, there he is." Molly points out to him.

I turn my head to look at this Max and gasp. No way.

Oh my god. How is that possible?

My Max, the one who broke my heart just walked through the doors, his once bright brown eyes were now dark and empty. His silky brown hair was unruly, it made him look mysterious but hot.

He still had his amazing build and sharp features. He looks like Max but at the same time, he doesn't. He looks here but not here.

I look away from him and quickly pack my stuff up. Molly gives me a look of confusion but copies me.

I need to get out of here, I need to get things under control.

I can't believe it's him. The guy I hate more than anything else.

I rush to the bins and dump my stuff up.

"Ava, what—"

"I need the toilet," I say, cutting her off and walking to the doors. I keep my head down just in case he'll see me. I don't want him to see me.

But apparently keeping my head down was a bad idea because I end up bumping into a hard chest. Strong arms wrap around my body; I feel sparks ignite, leaving me confused.

What?

Hesitantly, I look up and my eyes widen in shock as I see Max staring at me.

He seems shocked too. But he quickly recovers, his eyes tightening around me. I see disbelief and happiness in his eyes. Why is he happy?

Recovering from my shock, I try and get away from him, sending him a harsh glare.

"Ava?" He finally says, in disbelief.

5

5 | You Deserve Much Worse Than That

"Ava?" Max says, in disbelief.

My heart goes crazy at him saying my name again and I have to try hard to stop the shivers from going down my spine.

"Let go of me, Max," I demand, glaring at him.

Max looks a bit taken back at first but then his eyes narrow at me.

"No Princess, I don't want to."

I glower at him, trying to get out of his hold. "Its always what you want. Just let go of me."

"No." He growls out.

Ugh, not even 2 minutes in his presence and I already want to kill him.

I guess I'll have to find another way to get out. I internally smirk as I come up with an idea.

Stopping my struggles, I try to calm myself down.

Max looks at me with admiration and love. He looks like a man who has been deprived of water for a long time. He looks at me like I'm his salvation.

Whilst I look at him like I want to murder him. Which I do.

His eyes assess me, awe shining in them as he fully sees my face. He studies everything, engraving it in his mind.

Whilst he's distracted, I lift my leg up and knee him in the balls. Immediately, he lets go of me and I escape.

I step back to see Molly looking at us in confusion. She has no idea what's going on right now and to be honest, neither do I.

Why would Max look at me like that? He broke my heart, he ripped it out of my chest and crushed it. He should know I hate him. He shouldn't even like me, he ruined me.

"That wasn't nice princess." Max groans out, narrowing his eyes at me. I shrug my shoulders, not caring.

"You deserve much worse than that," I state.

"Ava, what I did that..."

"Don't even talk about it." I hiss and he stops, his eyes looking upset.

We stand there in silence, me glaring at him whilst Max gives me a hopeless expression. I notice Molly keeps glancing at the two of us, trying to work out what's going on.

"I still love you, Ava. What I did two years ago was..."

Once again, I cut Max off. "Let's go, Molly." And with that, I grab Molly and drag her off with me.

I can feel his eyes on me, watching me leave. I can also feel majority of the students here looking at me with curiosity. If they didn't know me before, they do now.

I glance at Molly to see her frowning at me. Once we make it out of the cafeteria, I let go of her and run a hand through my hair. I can't believe I just saw Max. That is one massive, horrible coincidence. What did I deserve for this to happen to me?

"Ava..." Molly softly says and I look at her. "What just happened?"

I sigh and walk over to a locker to lean on it. I think I need some support to keep me up.

"That was something I hoped would never happen." I coldly say, crossing my arms.

Molly sighs and bits her lip. "I need more than that."

I really want to tell Molly but I don't know how to. I've only told one person the full story about what happened two years ago. Instead, I kept it inside of me. that way, I thought I could forget about it and move on. Keeping it hidden, trying to forget it seemed like the best option. But now, now that I go to the same school as him, I don't even know what I'm going to do. I can't really forget now.

"Molly, I don't know how to..." I look at her defeated, tears on the verge of spilling. I can't believe I'm going to cry, especially after vowing I would never shed a tear over him again.

Molly rushes over to me and hugs me, her vanilla scent flooding my nose. It comforts me, her scent making me feel safe.

The tears start to escape my eyes, despite my efforts and trail down my cheeks. Not long after, I start to sob.

I absolutely hate crying but what I hate—no, despise—is crying in school. If a crowd of people start to walk past now, I will die in humiliation. If Max walks past now...

I don't even want to go there.

"Oh, Ava," Molly whispers into my shoulder, her voice sympathetic. "What happened to you?"

"My heart was broken," I mumble back when the sobs start to subside.

Not long after, Molly pulls away and gets something out of her pocket. With a small smile, she hands me a tissue and I thank her, gratefully.

Sniffling, I slide down the lockers onto the ground. This is a great first day. I make some nice friends, already hate my teachers and bump into the devil himself. Could this day get any better?

"I met him two years ago." I blurt out. "We were on holiday and..."

I tell Molly the key parts of the story and by the time I've finished, the bell goes. Luckily, the tears managed to dry and disappear. We get up as students start to go to their lessons and I hug her.

A slight weight was lifted off of my shoulders from telling her. I know I can trust her, just by the way she looked at me told me I had just found a close friend. I don't trust many people—thanks to Max—so I'm very surprised I trusted Molly. I guess we have a connection.

"Thank you," I announce and she looks at me in confusion, tilting her head to the side. "For listening to me, for being my best friend."

Molly's eyes light up and she gives me a massive smile. She looks ecstatic, beyond pleased and I feel nothing but pride for making her feel like that. She was there for me and I swear on my life I will be there for her.

I figured she doesn't have many girl friends, from my short time of interaction and time spent with her. In the lessons we had together, she only talked to me, her eyes fearful of the other girls.

She seemed more comfortable with the boys but I suspect that's because they're her brother's friends and because she knows them.

"Anytime, bestie." She giggles and hugs me again. This time for her though, not for me.

"See ya later." She waves and skips off, disappearing into the crowds.

Shaking my head at her giddy behavior, I go to my new locker to get my P.E. kit. I think Luke and Lawrence are in my class so I know I won't be alone. I have a feeling they're going to question me about Max earlier and I can tell you now, that I'm not looking forward to that.

I hope he's not in any of my classes. If he is, I know he'll try to talk to me and come up with some explanation. I don't know why he's even trying, he made it very clear that he doesn't want to be with me two years ago.

Does he plan on torturing me even more by coming up with sick plan to get me back?

That would just be messed up if he is.

Well, if he does try to, I will show him my displeasure for him. He will know that I, Ava O'Connor will forever hate him.

That I will never, ever be with him again. I will never fall for him again, look at him with love again, be with him again. Because I'm not the same girl anymore, I'm a strong girl who doesn't fall for playboys.

Especially ones like Max.

6

6 | They're Like Vultures

The gym is already busy when I got there. Some have already changed into their kit whilst others were just chilling on the benches.

I sigh. P.E. is not my favorite subject. I am not in the mood for this, especially after seeing that devil. He has completely shattered my mood. First day and I bump into him. Old memories have resurfaced that I'd rather leave buried.

Thanks, Max, thank you for taking me down memory lane.

I just need to get this over and done with, then its home time.

I walk over to the coach, to introduce myself and ask for my new kit. Unfortunately, they didn't deliver it to my new house so I have to pick it up here. Meaning, if it doesn't fit, I'm screwed.

The coach is busy setting some cones up when I get there. He seems pretty young, looking around 20-something. I must admit, he looks pretty hot. And I bet I'm not the only one who thinks that.

"Hi." I greet with a smile. He lifts his blue eyes up to me and gives me a warm smile.

"Hello, you must be the new student. Ava right?" He asks and I nod in response. "Right, you must be looking for your kit."

Once again, I nod and he leads me to his office.

"Do you like P.E. Ava?" He asks me, probably trying to make me feel more comfortable. You know what teachers are like, wanting to make new friends with you.

"Uh..." I drawl. "Not really sir, sorry?" I smile sheepishly.

He chuckles. "I like you. At least you were honest."

I shrug. "Honesty is the best policy."

"Wise words. Where did you get it from?"

"A film." He laughs whilst I give a small smile. What can I say? Films are educational.

"Well...here you are." He says, handing me my uniform. I take it, mumbling a thank you. "Continue watching those films, one of those mottos may help somebody one day."

I nod unsurely and head back off to the changing rooms. I'm not looking forward to this, at all. At least Lawrence is with me.

As soon as I walk into the girl's room, everybody looks at me. Swallowing, my grip on my kit tightens as I force my legs to walk over to a bench. A girl with red hair is stood there, with a small smile on my face.

Feeling a bit better at her small, friendly gesture, I place everything down.

"Will you lot stop staring at her like vultures? She's new, that's all." The redhead snaps and everyone quickly diverts their eyes.

"Thank you." I gratefully say. I hate people who stare at you and gossip like they know you. Its rude. If they have something, they should say it to my face—not behind my back.

She shrugs like its nothing. "Anytime. I'm Bree by the way."

She holds out her small pale hand and I gladly take it. She seems honest and nice. I could always do with more girl friends. Not that Molly isn't enough, its just its always nice to have lots of different friends.

"Ava."

"Well, its nice to meet you. Are you ready for P.E.?" She asks and I immediately shake my head.

"Hell no." She laughs at me.

"Me either. Can't stand it. Half the time, the girls are oogling one of the guys, especially the coach. Its gross." She scrunches her nose in disgust at the memories.

I can't disagree with her, I hate it at my old school.

"I know. What do you think we're doing?" I ask curiously. I'm praying its not dodgeball or running. Otherwise, I'll die.

"No clue."

The rest of the time spent in the changing rooms is spent with both of us playing 20 questions. Bree said she's quite new here too, she came here around eight months ago. Since then, she's steered away from most groups and has blended with the crowd. She wants some friends but she never could find people who could relate to her.

I tell her I would be friends with her and that she could join our group. I swear I see her eyes well up at that but I could have been imagining it. Bree looks like a tough chick who likes to keep things to herself so I wouldn't expect her to cry. But then again, I shouldn't stick to the stereotypes.

"Which season do you prefer?" I ask her as we walk out of the changing rooms.

She tilts her head up to look at me. Bree's a bit shorter than me, standing around 5"3. But from what she loses in height, she makes up in feistiness. Or so, that's what her parents said.

"Summer, duh. I can't stand the cold, I literally die. At least in summer, I can try and tan. Keyword: try." She huffs and I laugh. She's right though, Bree is as pale as a ghost. She's a pretty pale though, her skin almost looks like snow.

"I agree. I hate having to wear tonnes of layers. Oh, and freezing to death. My poor fingers." I shiver, just thinking about the freezing cold.

"Favourite word beginning with s." She says.

"Supercalifragilisticexpialidocious." I instantly reply. I've always loved that word, especially when I like to annoy my mom.

"Huh?" She asks, knitting her brows together.

I stop and turn to stare at her. Please tell me she knows where that word came from. But, all I see in her green orbs in confusion.

"Its from a film." I slowly say, hoping she'll catch onto it.

Mary Poppins was one of my favorite films as a child. I wished as a child that she would come to my door and take me away on her umbrella. I so wished I could go fly away somewhere.

"Ava, I have no idea what you're on about." I nearly facepalm at her. Somebody needs to movie educated. Mary Poppins is a classic and one of my favorites. We can't know each other unless she's seen it.

Don't judge—its a rule of mine.

"Mary Poppins. Its from freaking Mary Poppins!" I shout.

"What's from Mary Poppins?" Lawrence appears, asking. I jump like ten feet in fear. I can't deal with things like that, honestly. I'm awful when watching horror films.

"Lawrence." I hiss. "What the hell?"

Lawrence shrugs. His eyes move towards Bree, glancing at her with curiosity.

"Who's this?" He asks and I bit my lip. He better accept Bree otherwise I'll punch him in the face.

"Bree, my new friend," I tell him, coming to stand with her, looping my arm into hers.

"Cool, I'm Lawrence. Nice to meet you." Lawrence introduces himself, giving a charming smile.

Boys.

"You too." She replies, giving him a small smile. She doesn't look affected by his smile which shocks Lawrence. Guess he wasn't expecting another girl to turn down his charm.

Men these days need to learn that not everything revolves around them.

I start to drag Bree along when I see the coach shout for us to come in. Lawrence follows behind us, a cute frown still on his face.

"Right, so as a lot of you seem knackered, I'm going to make this lesson easy." A few people cheer at what he says, including me. "But I still expect you to put some effort into this lesson. All you have to do is complete the small workouts on this sheet. Work in groups or whatever, just get it done."

And with that, he makes us disperse. The coach seemed so chill about all of this, hardly caring about this lesson. He does realize nobody is going to do the work, right?

"Group?" I ask and the other two nod their heads. I force Lawrence to get the sheet whilst me and Bree go to sit on the benches. There is no way I'm going to willingly do the work.

A few seconds Lawrence brings back the sheet and I fill everything, making up the times and scores.

"Favourite song?" Bree asks me, her eyes also glancing at Lawrence to include him.

"No idea." Lawrence answers.

"Seriously?" Bree asks and he nods.

"What about you Ava?" She turns to ask me.

"Sign Of The Times," I tell her truthfully. I'm not a One Direction fan but I do like their separate songs. Sign Of The Times is so emotional, truthful it just pulls me in. I can't help but love it.

"Huh, I didn't see that coming," Lawrence smirks at me. Narrowing my eyes, I skillfully kick him.

"Don't judge, its a great song."

Lawrence holds his arms up in mock surrender. "Sure, sure."

I purse my lips but ignore him.

Bree and Lawrence begin to chat about something else whilst my mind goes off somewhere else. I still can't believe I saw Max, here.

Its still hard to fathom.

"Hey, is that Max? Why's he here? This isn't his class." Lawrence questions and my eyes dart to the doors, where Max is walking in.

Oh no. No. No. This can't be happening.

My eyes widen as I see him coming straight over here, his eyes set on me. His posture looks tense and rigid. His hair is swept to the side, looking messy but hot nonetheless.

Is he following me? I swear I'll kill him if he is.

Max eventually stops right in front of us, his eyes still set on me.

"Ava, we need to talk." He demands.

7

7 | I Think I'm The Star Of This Movie

"Ava, we need to talk," Max demands.

I glare at him for ordering me around. Who does he think he is? The King?

"I'm not going anywhere near you," I growl.

He huffs at me, running a hand through his brown hair.

"Please Ava, I want—no need—to explain." He pleads, begging. He thinks I'm going to fall for his act. How funny.

"I'm not listening to a word you say. You made everything very clear two years ago." I say coldly, maintaining my glare. "Now leave me alone."

Max's eye twitches slightly, a sign that he's agitated. Good, I'm winding him up.

My eyes glance over to Lawrence and Bree who are both looking between me and Max with curious eyes. I can almost see the wheels turning in their heads about what's going on.

I don't really want to explain everything again, telling my story once was heartbreaking. I don't think I can go through another emotionally exhausting story again today.

"Ava—"

"Go." I snap, interrupting him. Hopefully, he'll get the message. I doubt it but a girl can dream.

"No. I'm not leaving until I explain everything." He snaps back, straightening his posture. I purse my lips in annoyance, narrowing my eyes. Can't he just leave me alone? He's already tortured me enough, my heart just can't take anymore.

"Listen here, Max." I start, standing up so that I'm my full height. Even though I only reach his chin, I'm still pretty tall. "I don't want to do this again. I got the message okay?"

My voice turns slightly softer at the end from my sadness. My mind keeps replaying it over and over, to make me feel worse.

"I know and I'm sorry but what you saw—"

I cut him off again. "I know what I saw so don't come up with some bullshit excuse okay?"

He looks upset that I won't listen to him yet he continues. I know Max, he won't give up. Or, at least, that's what he used to be like.

"Ava." He sighs, annoyed. "I'm not trying to make an excuse. I know what you saw and I'm trying to say that what you saw didn't happen."

Biting the inside of my cheek, I try to tell if he's lying. His eyes stare into mine, holding it. The desperation for me to believe him is unreal. He seems so lost; broken. A small part of me pity's him but before I even think about giving some sort of pity, I remember the heartbreak. He doesn't deserve my sympathy. He ruined me—changed me; I'll never forgive him for that. Not ever.

"I miss you. I made a mistake and I will forever hate myself for it." His tone is desperate. His eyes are pleading with me to acknowledge him in a way that isn't hate. He wants redemption. "I need you, Ava."

Hearing those words pulls at something in my heart. He needs me but do I need him?

No, I hate him. I remind myself, scolding myself for even thinking about wanting him. I've moved on, I'm different now.

Anger boils in me at his words instead. It's a way for me to hide the fact I even thought about needing him.

How could he say that? After what he put me through, he doesn't deserve my forgiveness.

So, me being the impulsive person I am, I slap him. Hard.

Max looks stunned, his eyes wide open in shock as he raises a hand to feel his cheek. Satisfaction floods through me as I see my handy work.

"You have no right to say that to me. Not after what you put me through." I say, taking a step back. Glancing at Bree and Lawrence I see them staring at us in shock. I guess they didn't think I would slap him.

I'm also assuming they didn't think I would have the guts to smack the 'bad boy'. They have no idea what's going on so I dread to think where their minds are taking them. Worse case scenario: somewhere that involves crime. Hopefully.

"Now, leave me alone," I repeat, grabbing Bree's arm. I drag her away from Max to the changing rooms, ignoring some of the other student's eyes who are on me. I just gave them something to gossip about. Wonderful.

Bree doesn't question me, just letting me pull her to the changing rooms. The frown her face lets me know she's curious and that I should probably expect some questions from her. I honestly don't know what to tell her, I could tell her the truth or I could say I don't feel like answering right now. I'm sure she'd understand.

After all, all I want to do now is curl up in a whole and drown in my sorrows. Well, that and laugh at how pathetic my life has become. Fate is so cruel or was it my luck? If anything else boy related happens to me here, right now, I could be the star of my own TV show. That, or if a jealous girl who claims Max is hers approaches me and 'threatens' me, I will go and see a movie producer and force him to make a movie about me.

Not kidding.

Slamming the door open, I let go of Bree's arm and collapse onto one of the seats. This is all overwhelming. Seeing Max, telling my story and now having Max come up with excuses is all too much for me.

Leaning my head back closing my eyes taking a deep breath to try and calm down. I need to get everything back under control like I had it before.

"Ava, I know you probably don't want to talk about what happened back there but if you ever do—want to talk—just know that I will always listen." Bree's soft and comforting voice fills my ears.

I'm grateful to know that she'll always be here for me if I ever need to open up. Its reassuring to know.

"Thank you," I say, gratitude clear in my voice. "You didn't ask me questions and for that I'm grateful. Oh and for also telling me you'll be here. Its...I don't know. It's just nice to know that you'll be there if I need you."

"Anytime." She chirps, sitting down next to me.

I open my eyes and give her a small smile. She returns it with bright green eyes.

"So." Bree nervously starts, tucking a bit of her red hair behind her ear. "I know this nice place that does coffee and hot chocolates if you wanna go there after school."

I ponder over it. Spending time with Bree would be nice, that way we can get to know each other.

"Sure. Can we bring Molly too? I bet she'd love to meet you." I ask, smiling at the thought of all of us being friends. Inviting her would mean they would get to meet and we would have a small circle of girls to be friends with. I want to be friends with both of these girls; I want them to be friends too. Otherwise, it would be weird and awkward if I had to meet them separately and spend time with them separately.

"Of course." She beams excitedly.

Her happiness is contagious—I swear—because my bad mood deteriorates and I just can't help but smile happily back at her.

"Yay," I cheer. Then, not even a second later, the bell goes off and the girls come in. Wiping the smile off of my face, I get up and go over to my bag. Sneaking a small smile at Bree.

I don't want to draw attention to myself, smiling like a madman isn't something else I want to add to the gossip. Half of these girls are giving me death glares as well, whilst a few of the blonde clones are giving me disgusted looks as their eyes roam my body.

They must be cheerleaders, judging by their forms and the clothing they're changing into. They also look like people from the popular group, if the way some quieter girls are sneaking glances at them enviously.

So now, not only do I have Max to deal with but also, I have some nasty looking cheerleaders to deal with who look like they want to bite my head off.

What's the number for a producer? I'm sure a movie about my life would be a hit. I can tell a lot of juicy drama is coming for me, perfect for a teen movie.

8

8 | Carpool Karaoke

Striding through the halls with Bree, my eyes search for Molly. I'm hoping she'll agree to coffee with us, I could do with some friendly bonding. Seeing as I only started at this school today, I'd like to say I'm doing a pretty well friends wise. So far, I've met two nice girls who want to be friends with me.

And it only took me one day! One day for me to have made friends who seem like true friends.

"Where do you think she'll be?" Bree asks me, also searching for Molly. Bree hasn't officially met Molly yet so she has no idea what she looks like so she's only going on what I told her. Which was a brief description of how pretty she looks.

Eventually, I spot Molly's long and silky black hair in the crowd, talking to Dan. Grabbing Bree's hand, I drag her over.

"Molly!" I call and she turns her head to look at me.

"Hey." She smiles, her eyes looking at me then to Bree. She looks confused, as her eyes scan me, then Bree and then back to me. I hope she doesn't over-think something crazy.

"Phew, I thought I'd lost you for a second," I exclaim, stopping in front of her and Harry. I don't fail to notice how Harry's eyes linger on Bree, his brown eyes assessing her up and down.

I let go of Bree's arm and step forward to hug Molly.

Stepping back from Molly, I grab Bree's shoulders and bring her forwards. "I want you to meet Bree, my new friend. She kind of saved me in P.E. earlier."

Giving the siblings a small smile, she waves. "Hi."

"Hi, Bree." Molly nicely says, beaming at Bree. "It's nice to meet you, I'm Molly." Molly then hugs Bree, momentarily surprising her. Bree freezes for a second until she realizes Molly's a nice person, making her relax.

Molly, still grinning ear-to-ear, moves away from Bree and lets Harry introduce himself. Giving a charming smile, he holds out his hand. "Josh."

"Cool," Bree mutters, her eyes moving to the ground. Harry's smile falters but he keeps it nonetheless. He gives me a questioning look and I just shrug. How would I know what's going on? I met Bree a few hours ago.

The way Harry's gazing her right now though, tells me that Bree might be uncomfortable around Harry. I feel some sort of sexual tension around them. Could there possibly be an...attraction?

Could Harry, possibly like Bree? But how, don't they like barely know each other? Unless...

I glance at Bree to see her eyes briefly flicker up to Harry and an unrecognizable emotion flashes in her green eyes. She then drops her head down again, kicking her shoe on the ground like its the most interesting thing ever.

"Right then." I clear my throat, trying to ease the weird piece of tension between Bree and Harry. "Do you ladies want to get a hot chocolate or Coffee? Whatever it is at that place you said, Bree."

"Mama Coco's." She informs me and I nod.

"Yeah, sure." Molly smiles brightly and hugs Harry, whispering a goodbye to him. Harry stares at Bree one last time before trotting off to god knows where. Molly then grabs onto my arm and Bree's and leads us out of the school.

"Right so, do any of you have a car?" I ask them and they both shake their heads.

"I normally get a ride from Josh," Molly tells me.

"I normally walk." Bree answers.

"Okay, good." I chirp. "Luckily, I have a car."

I unlock my car and get into the driver's seat whilst Molly hops into the other front seat and Bree gets into the back middle seat. "Now, I have some ground rules when you're in this car," I announce.

Unsurely, Molly nods.

"Right so, EATING is strictly forbidden in this car. If my dad thinks I'm not looking after it, he'll literally ban me from it for a month." I tell them, sighing as I remember that one time my dad made me listen to a thirty-minute lecture on how I have to take care of the car. He spent a lot of his 'hard-working' money on it so he doesn't want it ruined. "Also, I choose the music. I don't want any rubbish music, got it?"

They both nod their heads again, almost robotically.

Sighing, I rub my forehead. "Sorry, dad's orders. He can be really strict when it comes to his 'precious' cars."

Molly shrugs. "Its okay, Josh can be the same for his car. He once had this rule that if anyone went close to his precious Caroline that they would have their heads chopped off."

Chuckling, I shake my head in amusement. What is it with boys and their cars?

Turning on the ignition, I flick through the radio station to find something good. Eventually, one station has an old Miley Cyrus song.

Behind me, Bree squeals. "Oh my gosh, I love this song. I remember dancing to it all of the time in front of the mirror."

"Yes, same!" Molly smiles. "Honestly though, I still do that."

"To be fair, don't we all do that from time to time?" I add and we all laugh, knowing its true.

"So I put my hands up, I'm playing my song and I'm doing my own good thing." We all sing as I start to reverse out. When I look forward, I see Max standing in front of a Porshe, his eyes set on my car. On me. His intense gaze is sending shivers down my spine; all it makes me want to do is continue to get lost in his beautiful eyes.

Stop!

Gulping, I try and ignore his gaze as I quickly get out of the school car park. I need to forget about him. Max is a man-whore who broke your heart. He doesn't deserve your attention.

Listening to my subconscious, I tune back into the song, humming whilst the girl's full-on sing. Unfortunately, they can't sing. They sound worse then my Nan and she's ninety.

"Guys, guys!" I shout over the music, getting their attention. "Please, maybe not sing as loud? You two sound like foghorns."

Bree and Molly share a look before bursting out in laughter. My cheeks slightly turn pink and I have to shake my head so my light brown hair will cover it up.

"Foghorns?" Bree asks through her fits of laughter. "Oh my gosh, where did you get that from?"

I roll my eyes. My mom used to tell me I sound like a fog horn when I would sing in the car or in the Kitchen with her.

"My mom."

"Wow." Molly giggles. "Your mom must really love you."

Deciding to have my own fun, I answer back in a really bad southern accent. "She sure does."

This time, we all burst out in laughter. These two girls give me loads of happiness; they make this place feel like home again. Sure, I'm going to miss my old friends but these two make me feel like I can be happy here too. Minus Max.

Max can go and screw himself. He broke my heart and abandoned me, I don't need him. Like my dad says, if a guy could even think about another woman whilst in love with you, he isn't worth your time. A true man who loves you will always be devoted to you.

"Okay, so I have no idea where we're going. Can someone give directions?" I ask once I've sobered up.

"Um...you just turned the passing for it," Bree tells me and I groan. Great.

"Is there another turning?" I ask her, hoping she says the next one is coming up soon.

"The next one is in like ten minutes," Molly says, causing me to groan again.

I really want a hot chocolate. I haven't had one in what feels like forever - saying that, I actually had one last week at Starbucks. Man, I love Starbucks.

"At least we get to chat more and listen to music." Molly shrugs just as Ignition comes on.

Smiling, I turn the volume up and let the windows drop as we all sing like maniacs. With the wind blowing our hair and the girls laughing whilst singing, I feel great. I wish everything could be just like this.

9

9 | He's Max, Max The Stalker

"This place is so cute." I muse to the two girls as we step into the old cafe. Observing it, I notice how it has a bookshelf full of books, little tables with flowers on them and some sofa's so you can sit casually and talk.

An old lady is stood behind the counter, fixing up the cakes. As soon as we walk over to the counter, she stands up straight, giving us a warm smile. She looks like she's in her mid 50's, with shiny gray hair and bright green eyes.

"Bree! Lovely to see you again. Are these two beautiful ladies your friends?" She curiously asks, giving us joyful smiles. This woman has an aura of kindness around her, she seems like the type of person that can make you smile or laugh no matter what kind of day it is.

"Hi Grace, these two are my new friends. Molly and Ava." Bree answers her.

Grace nods her head. "Well hello. I'm Grace, owner of Mama Coco's. What do you all want to drink?"

I exam the menu above her on the wall, deciding I just want an ordinary hot chocolate.

"I'll have a hot chocolate please," I tell her, getting my money out. Molly orders the same as me.

"I'm guessing you want your usual Bree?" Grace asks her and Bree nods. We all pay Grace and she then insists we go and sit down whilst she makes them.

Bree leads us to one of the big sofa's and I plonk myself down, sighing at how comfortable it feels. I want one of these sofas in my bedroom.

"Here you are ladies," Grace says, carrying a tray that has our hot chocolates on. Thanking her again when she puts it on the table, I take a sip of it and moan at the taste. I've never had a hot chocolate before that tastes this good.

Bree was right, this is the best.

"Jeez, I think I just had an orgasm from this," Molly says, closing her eyes as she takes another sip.

Me and Bree both exchange looks and laugh at her.

"What? It's really good." Molly protests, pouting as we laugh harder.

"Sure." I laugh.

"Haha, really funny," Molly grumbles under her breath, rolling her eyes.

"To be honest, these are the best." Bree pipes up. We all agree at that.

We all talk for a bit, discussing things like life-long friends do. It feels like we've known each other forever.

"Psst, Ava, four o'clock," Molly whispers, sitting up on her couch opposite me.

I give Molly a confused look, about to look over my shoulder when Molly gives me a kick under the table.

"Hey! That hurt." I whisper-yell, rubbing my poor leg. Who knew Molly could give such a powerful kick.

Bree gives Molly a confused look too until she looks over to where Molly was on about and opens her mouth in realization. What or who is it? If its a celebrity like Beyonce, I'm so getting her autograph.

I doubt Beyonce will be somewhere like here but that's not going to stop me from dreaming. Every. Single. Night.

"Okay, guys, who is it? What's going on?" I inquire, raising an eyebrow.

Bree leads forwards. "Your least favorite person."

My least favorite person? Cryptic much.

Giving a name will make my life so much easier.

Giving Bree an expected look to continue she sighs and tells me. Immediately, my head snaps to the side and I do see the handsome devil, who is observing the cakes. He must feel my eyes on him because his beautiful chocolate eyes look up to meet mine and plead with me to give him a chance.

Like hell, I will. Break my heart once, shame on you. Try to break my heart again, that's a big mistake.

"Great," I mutter under my breath, giving Max a glare before turning back to the girls who are wearing guilty faces. "Not your fault, it's just a coincidence he's here. Right?"

Bree and Molly swap looks; hesitantly nod heads. Totally not helping guys.

Sighing, I pray Max doesn't come over here for round three. It appears nobody's on my side today because he comes over to me. Like why? What did I do to deserve this? I've done everything right in life, couldn't I just have this one time?

"Ava, please can I talk to you?" He begs, standing to the side with his hands in his pockets.

"No Max, just leave me alone," I demand.

"I can't. What happened that day isn't what you think, I still lo -"

"I saw what happened that day." I snap, standing up, walking over to him. "You broke my heart. No, you ripped it out of my chest." I non-humorously laugh. "Don't, ever, say I miss-saw it because I know I didn't."

Max shuts his gob at that, a regretful look on his face. I nearly scoff at it, like he would regret breaking my heart. Boys like him do things like this for fun. Not caring about the consequences or how the girl feels. It's all just a game to them.

I've seen it happen before to my fellow friends, I've seen how devastated they are. I know how devastating it is.

"Goodbye Max." I emotionlessly say, leaving no room for further discussion, sitting back on the sofa. I've said everything I needed to say.

Apparently, Max doesn't agree with me though.

"Ava, I'm not leaving until I explain myself. I want – no need - you back. What happened that day will forever haunt me as one of the worst days of my life. I hurt you and by hurting you, I hurt me too. I love you, Ava. I realized that the second I lost you."

Speechless, I just sit there, processing what he said. Max still loves me? After everything, he did to me? If you love someone you don't cheat on them. If you really loved them, you just physically couldn't.

"Liar," I claim.

Max shakes his head. "This is straight from my heart. I am still crazy in love with you."

"I refuse to believe you," I say. "Please just leave me alone now. I don't want to see you again."

From the corner of my eye, I can see Max's defeated look. I don't care though, he ruined me. He's just saying he loves me to try and win my sympathies. I'm not going to fall for it again.

Max walks away, his shoulders slumped and his head hung low. He exits the cafe, casting a final look at me.

I look away before we can make eye contact, I don't want to see his pleading eyes. I fear that if I see them, I will give into him.

Sighing, I lean back on the sofa, enjoying his comfort. Max might have finally received the message; now he will leave me alone. At least, that's what I'm hoping.

"Ava, don't you think you're being a bit harsh on Max?" Bree asks me, glancing at the door Max just left through.

"Hell no. Max made me fall for him, hard and then he cheated on me. He showed off his victory right in front of me." I coldly answer. "He deserves every horrible thing I say to him."

Bree closes her mouth, giving me an apologetic look as she takes a sip of her hot chocolate.

"You know." Molly starts, crossing her left leg over her right. "After that summer two years ago, he changed. He genuinely looks upset and guilty about what went down. Do you not maybe think you could give him a chance to at least explain himself?"

"I don't think I would be able to restrain myself from strangling him for that long," I admit and they laugh.

"Hey, I have a brilliant idea," Bree announces. I raise an eyebrow at her. She clears her throat and starts. "Well, since he clearly won't leave you alone, maybe you should send him a message."

I tilt my head to the side. Send a message, huh? Hmm.

"What do you have in mind?"

"Well, I know Max loves his car, maybe as much as he 'loves' you." Bree puts 'loves' in air quotes. "How about we wreck something that's precious to him to show that if you really were precious to him, that's how it felt for you. You know, make him feel what you feel. Anger, hurt, sadness etc."

I like where Bree's going with this. This is like a little revenge plan.

"Bree, you're a genius." I compliment her, smirking at both of the girls. Molly also grins like a madman, it's obvious she's never been in a revenge plot like this before.

Let's just say, after Max, I went through a rough period where I sort of rebelled against the teachers at my old school and pranked some of the bitchy students. In all fairness, a lot of them deserved what they got.

"Let's do this." Molly giggles, pumping her fist into the air. Bree and I just laugh at her silliness; start devising a plan.

Max is so going to regret harming me. He's going to regret even glancing at me.

Because nobody messes with Ava. Nobody.

10

10 | Revenge Is A Dish Best Served Cold

"Okay, so maybe we shouldn't do this." Molly comments, nervously biting her lip as she observes the car we are planning to destroy.

Bree waves her hand in a dismissive manner. "Nah, I think he deserves this. What do you think Ava?"

I don't immediately reply, my mind too focused on Max's car in front of me. I'm so going to be killed if my parents find out about that I even planned to do this.

"Uh..." I trail off, unsure of how to answer. On the one hand, it did feel good. Really good. But...on the other hand, I'm be murdered for this. My parents are going to flip, kill me by accident and then will invite the wrong people to the funeral. I bet they will even put the wrong flowers out and they will probably end up going down to the local pub to 'celebrate' my life.

You may think I'm overreacting but I'm not. Really, I'm not.

"Well," I clear my throat, "it would be nice to get revenge but you see...the thing is...I don't want to get in trouble."

Bree gives me a look of disbelief whilst Molly raises her hand up as if to say 'thank you for making sense.'

"Oh come on! What's the chance of your parents finding out?" Bree raises an eyebrow.

"Pretty high," I mutter with a sigh. My parents were really good friends with their parents and I bet if they saw each other again, they would rekindle it. Thus, they talk and walla, my parents find out.

"How would they find out?" Molly curiously asks me.

"They're really good friends with Max's parents," I tell her. Molly's mouth makes an 'o' shape whilst Bree kicks a pebble on the ground.

"Well then...maybe we shouldn't?" Molly unsurely glances at me and then Bree. Personally, I want to do more than reck Max's car but I don't want my parents finding out. They might finally send me to that Switzerland school that Aunt Rosie was always going on about.

"It's up to Ava, after all, it will affect her the most." Bree shifts the attention to me. Now, I have been known to be that person who makes the worst decisions. So, for me to be the one to decide what happens is not a good idea. I don't think the decision being revenge on the guy who broke my heart and messed me up should be something I decide.

I really, really want to get some payback but I'm also terrified of the effects. Do I want to take the revenge?

Yes? No? Yes? No?

Yes.

"Let's do this," I say determinedly, my eyes staying on the vehicle.

Bree squeals whilst Molly sucks in s breath anxiously. I know this isn't her thing and she won't want to back out in fear of humiliation but I don't want to be that friend who puts peer pressure on other friends. I'm not that type of person.

"Hey Mol," I whisper to her whilst Bree starts getting the fish out. "You sure you want to do this? I'd understand if you wanted to leave, Bree too."

Molly bits her lip, glancing at the car and me. She has an apprehensive look on her face, as she starts running a hand through her dark hair. "I want to do this, for you."

I nod my head my heart soaring at the fact that this girl who has known me for one day wants to help me out.

I open Max's door and grab the baby oil out of my bag. I wipe it all over his steering wheel with pride. I don't feel a tad amount of remorse for doing this, we deserve this.

Once I've finished with that, I get out my spray paint. Might as well let Max know who did this, he would work it out eventually.

I spray Payback's a b*tch on his car, smirking at my masterpiece. Molly comes around the car to look at it, her brown eyes wide in shock. Bree comes around the other side and rests her arm on my shoulder.

"Nice work." She compliments. "We should probably get out of here now."

With that, we all sprint away from his car and hop into my car.

"Wow, that was..." Molly starts.

"Exhilarating, amazing, the best kind of revenge you've ever done." Bree finishes the sentence, sending a cheeky smile to Molly over her shoulder.

Molly shrugs. "I was going to say rushed but okay. Same-ish thing."

I roll my eyes and speed out. I feel like such a rebel right now. I don't regret doing it though, this was long overdue.

"Right, who lives closer?" I ask them. Time to go home.

***

As I walk through my new school the next day, I notice pupils whispering to each other. They're all wearing worried looks and all of them keeping glancing at the main doors.

I spot Molly and the rest of the gang and head over there.

"Ava! So lovely to see you again." Luke cheers, approaching me for a hug. Quickly noticing what he's about to do, I dodge his advance causing everyone to laugh whilst he gives me a pout. "That's not very nice, I was only trying to be friendly."

"Sure..." I sarcastically drawl. "Anyway, what's got everybody watching the main doors like hawks? Is a celebrity visiting or something?"

"Oh, Max's car was vandalized last night so when he turned up to school today, he was furious. He's been snapping at everybody who tries to talk to him. Everyone's anxiously waiting for him to step into school." Josh explains. My eyes widen, along with Molly's and Bree's.

Now, this is the part I'm not going to enjoy.

"On a scale of one to ten, ten being very, very angry. How angry would you say he is?" I nervously ask them. I'm happy I haven't bumped into him but I'm dreading it when I do. I can almost imagine how bad that encounter is going to go.

"Oh, a definite ten," Josh answers with certainty. Great.

Faintly, I hear a door bash and open and some gasps. Oh god, I know what's going to happen.

From my peripheral vision, I see a very angry Max storm over to me. The others give me curious looks, except for Molly and Bree who know all about it. They seem a bit scared too but know Max has no idea they joined in. He only knows it was me.

People part for Max as he marches over to me, his eyes staying on me.

He stops a few inches away from me, close enough for me to be able to smell his cologne. I've always liked his smell, weird but its rather appealing.

"Sweetie, can we talk in private?" He surprisingly asks calmly, a contradiction to his current facial expression. I don't what I'd prefer, an angry Max or a calm one. They're both equally scary.

I glare at the pet name. "No." I stubbornly say, lifting my chin up slightly.

Max gives me a frustrated look, clenching his jaw. "Now."

I shake my head. "I'm not going anywhere with you. Now leave me alone."

"Ava, I'm losing my patience." He grits out, stepping a bit closer.

"Aww, poor you," I smirk at his warning look. "Now go."

"This is your last warning babe. If you don't come willingly, then I'll find another way for you to come." I ignore his wicked smile and stand my ground.

Max's eyes light up at my response. One minute he was all temperamental and now he's all smiles. Is he bipolar or something?

"Fine then, don't say I didn't warn you."

"What—" I start but I'm interrupted as Max bends down and grabs my knees.

Hoisting me into the air like I weigh nothing, I'm thrown over his shoulder.

"Max!" I screech, thrashing in his hold. He can't seriously be doing this? In school! He's mad! Bonkers.

Max begins walking away, with everyone watching gawking at the situation. I look at them, pleading with them to help me.

Nobody does, I guess they're frightened by Max's harsh glare that he's giving them. Don't ask me how I know he's glaring, I just do.

"Put me down right now," I demand angrily.

Max's shoulders shake as he chuckles. He's laughing. Freaking laughing. Unbelievable.

Nobody would think he's carrying a girl over his shoulder unless they saw it. Which they are and yet, they aren't doing anything. What has society come to?

"This is kidnapping." Yes, I have resorted to that. Its the only other solution I can think of since my demands are not going registering in his head.

"Well if it is, I'm your knight in shining armor." He jokes and I smack his back.

"Oh please, your the ugly, evil villain who is kidnapping the innocent young girl," I reply, rolling my eyes.

Max laughs at that and then he turns fake gasps. "How dare you! I'm not ugly! I'm very handsome and sexy."

I purse my lips together. Of course, that's what he gets all defensive about. Doesn't mention how he is kidnapping me. A semi—innocent girl.

"Still as conceited, egotistical and narcissistic as you were two years ago," I mumble under my breath.

Finally, Max comes to a halt. He opens a door and walks us into it, without any lights on. Shutting the door, he drops me onto the ground and turns on a light.

My eyes wander around the small closet and I give him a glare. He brought me to the freaking janitors closet! How original.

"Why did you bring me here?" I ask, crossing my arms. "Do you want to introduce me to the janitor or something? Oh no wait"

Max leans against the wall, observing me. He has that same smirk on his face that he had the day we met. It's not as good as his smile but its good enough to get my heart thumping in my chest.

"Still over—thinking things I see," he comments. I shrug and lean against the opposite side of the wall.

"Why did you bring me here?" I bring the important matter back. Max rolls his eyes at my question again and then gives me a ghost smirk. I glower at him, making him raise his hands up in mock surrender.

Max sighs. "You know why. You recked my car. A car I love, not as much as you but one I still love."

I snort. "That's cringey."

"But true," he sighs.

My stomach does a U-turn as it drives crazy. He can't just say that so...casually. Like he's saying he had Pizza for tea last night.

"If you want me to apologize. News flash, it's not going to happen."

"I know." He says. "I know you better than you know yourself."

He thinks he knows me better than myself but he doesn't. He might know the old me but this me, he doesn't know. I've changed. Ava from two years ago is very different from Ava today. Nad honestly, I don't even know myself.

"You don't. Now let me go." I command.

"Not until we talk." It appears we are going to be in here for a long time. A very long time.

11

11 | The Truth Hurts Sometimes

Twenty minutes after being kidnapped by Max, I'm still here waiting to be released. After the argument we had continued to go on an endless cycle, I decided I would just shut my mouth and wait until he gets fed up with the silent treatment. He should then release me.

"You know the longer you stay silent, the longer you stay in here with me." Max attempts to get me talking again. "This is really immature, you're acting like my five—year—old cousin."

I still ignore him. I've been leaning against the wall for a while now, trying to keep some distance between us. This closet is really tiny making it hard to keep space between us. I hate to admit it but when I'm close to him, I feel all of those emotions that I had two years ago. Its confusing as hell, I hate the guy yet I still feel the attraction, the pull between us.

He broke my heart; I'm still having butterflies when I'm close to him.

Damn you, Max.

He frustratedly tugs a hand through his brown hair, shooting an annoyed look my way. I mentally smirk at what I'm doing to him—I'm finally getting on his nerves!

"Ava, please," he begs. "Please just answer me, just give me some sort of response. I need to tell you what happened two years ago. Its been driving me insane. What you saw wasn't what you think, please."

Lies. Lies. Lies. I know what I saw two years ago, I have eyes. I saw it perfectly well, he's trying to change my views. What is it they say?

Fool me once, shame on you. Fool me a second time...

"Goddammit, woman, just listen to me for five minutes, if you still want to hate me and never see me again then fine. I will accept that and will leave you alone." Max offers, his face not looking pleased at all by the last bit.

Hmm, is it worth it? I mean, I only have to listen to him produce some pitiful, well—rehearsed excuse and then I can go. He will then leave me alone for the rest of my time here.

Easy right? Only five minutes of my time for the rest of my life.

"Fine," I agree, biting my lip.

Max exhales with relief like he thought I wouldn't take up his offer and would continue to ignore him.

"You have five minutes starting from now," I announce. I'm going to count down in my head seeing as I can't be bothered to go on a hunt for my phone that is somewhere in my bag.

"Right so, what you saw didn't actually happen." He starts and I roll my eyes. You've already said that a dozen times. Max must have noticed my irritated look because he shoots me a glare and continues, "it was a setup."

Huh? Did I hear him right? A setup? That doesn't make any sense. Why would he set up being with another girl?

I was expecting a pre-planned fake excuse but this is just lame. I mean, come on Max! Come up with something more believable.

I open my mouth in shock but then close it again, trying to comprehend what he said. Why would it be a setup? That doesn't make any sense. I mean, who even does that?

"Yeah, right," I snort. I'm not going to fall for that.

Max gives me another annoyed look. He rubs his face with his hands angrily. I haven't noticed until now how tired he looks. He looks exhausted. Is he mentally tired? Physically tired? Or both?

"Ava, its true. I set it up because I was stupid. I don't know how to explain it...what we had was amazing. You knew it, I knew it but I had to mess it up. I thought it was too good to be true. I mean, I fell for you so hard Ava, I literally had to be with you once a day. It was crazy and it didn't feel healthy.

"So I did something stupid, something I will regret for the rest of my life. I hired some girl who was staying at the hotel to come in a t-shirt and to eat breakfast with me. I told her to make it look like we were together. As soon as she stepped into the room, I knew it was a mistake but I still went through with it. We didn't do anything though, she came into the room in the morning and pretended to take an interest in me. But I hated it, I hated touching her."

What? I—I don't know what to say. That's messed up. I get that he was scared but he could have literally done anything else. He could have come to me and told me about it—we could have talked it out together. What he did was cruel.

Why out of everything he could have chosen, did he do that?

Max takes a deep breath and continues, "and then I got that letter. As soon as I read it, I forced her to leave. It broke my heart Ava, I knew I hurt you which made me feel so upset. I was angry at myself for what I did to you. I prayed every day that I would see you so that I could apologize and get you back. I thought about you every second. I love you so much."

Collapsing onto the cold ground, I register everything he said. Did I really cause him pain by the thought of me being in pain?

This is crazy.

We are both in silence, me on the floor letting everything sink in whilst Max is deep in thought. He is wearing a nervous expression, I assume because he fears I will either not believe him or I will tell him to leave me alone for good.

"Please say something Ava," Max breaks the silence whilst running a hand through his hair. It looks messy, messier than usual because he's been running a hand through it a lot.

"What do you want me to say?" I snap back at him. Max gives me a shocked look, clearly not expecting me to give him an aggressive answer. "Sorry," I breathe out. "I—I don't know what to say. This is a massive bombshell, I'm in shock. Give me a few more minutes."

I didn't expect Max to agree but he must have thought about the position I'm in because he nods and falls to the ground as well.

He pretended to cheat on me because he was scared about our relationship so he thought by doing that it would end and he wouldn't have to worry. Stupid, very stupid I know. I'm glad he can admit that it was a massive mistake but I'm still not happy about his tactics. If he had just talked to me about his fear then we wouldn't be here right now.

The question is, do I want to forgive him? Can I put that heartbreaking and traumatic moment past me and forgive him? Can we even go back to a relationship after this?

I could but if I let him back in my life, he could hurt me again.

Ugh, I don't know what to do! One the one hand, me and Max could potentially go back to what we had but on the other hand, he could break my heart. Goddammit!

I sigh and bring my legs closer to my chest so that I can hug myself. Max watches all of my movements like a hawk, not once straying his eyes away from me.

"Max—"

"Before you tell me your decision, just know that I really am sorry and I love you so much. The past two years have been awful. It's pitiful how I acted, I was like a zombie. Screw people who say true love doesn't exist. I know it does exist because you're my true love." He cuts me off with a pleading speech. He wants me to forgive him, so much.

My heart is hammering in my chest just by the look he's giving me. He resembles a lost puppy who only wants love. Wow, has it really resorted to this?

"If I do forgive you, what will you do?" I ask him.

He gives me a longing look, "I will win your heart back."

"Why?! Why won't you just let me go?" I ask, a part of me outraged that he thinks we can come back whilst another part is giddy. I'm so confused, I feel so conflicted.

"Because" he simply shrugs.

"Because?" I repeat with an expected look. He can't just say because and not justify anything.

"Because I'm finding Ava, I'm finding you," He truthfully answers, his brown orbs staring into my blue orbs.

12

12 | To Forgive Or Not, That Is The Question

"Because I'm finding Ava, I'm finding you," He truthfully answers, his brown orbs staring into my blue orbs.

"Y—You can't just say stuff like that Max. It's not fair to me, you're making me feel confused." I tell him whilst trying to comprehend what he said. Doesn't he understand that the old me is gone? I disappeared the second he broke my heart.

Max releases a frustrated sigh and tugs his hand through his brown hair, "I know but I wanted to be truthful. I want you back Ava."

I didn't reply to his comment.

Shortly after that, Max left, promising he would fix me. I don't know how long I stayed in the janitors closet thinking but when the janitor angrily came in and shouted at me for being here, I scrambled out. I guess he didn't appreciate me being in his 'private' space.

I check the time and nearly face plant the floor. I missed the first period! Max, you asshole! My biology teacher isn't somebody you mess with if yesterday was anything to go by. She is actually going to strangle me or chain me to the table and make me do everything I missed.

The second period has already begun so I decide to skip it and go off to the library. I could do with some study time.

I hum as I head over to the library at the end of the building and sneak in. There are a few other students here revising, some of them look up and some ignore me. I shrug and sit down at an empty table far away from everyone else.

And with that, I start revising.

A text message knocks me out of my dedicated study time. I fish out my phone and unlock it.

From: Molly

To: Ava

Where are you? Been looking 4 you. Meet me in Maths period 3.

Crap! I have two minutes until Maths starts. I groan, annoyed with myself for not setting a timer. If I had, I wouldn't be rushing right now.

With my speedy typing skills, I send a reply to Molly telling her I will be there as soon as possible.

I sprint through the hallways, grunting every time I bashed into somebody. Some would protest and others would just give me annoyed looks. Teenagers.

Eventually, I see Molly leaning against the door outside of the classroom. Her hands are crossed over her chest as she stares at me.

"Hello," I greet with a smile, my face no doubt flushed from running.

Molly raises an eyebrow, "what happened to you? And why weren't you in biology earlier? Were you with Max?"

Damn, straight to the point.

I sigh and walk into the classroom with Molly behind me. I find a seat in the middle of the classroom and Molly sits next to me. After getting her folder out, Molly turns to fully face me.

"Ava, what happened? After Max kidnapped you, I didn't hear anything else from anyone."

"Well, Max locked me in the janitors closet," I tell her. Her brown eyes widen in shock and worry. She opens her mouth ready to fire questions at me but I cut her off, "its fine. We just needed to talk. He told me what happened two years ago; then he started begging me to give him a second chance."

Molly gasps, "really?"

I nod my head, "yeah so in other words, I told him that I don't do second chances. Then he proceeded to tell me that he's going to 'find' me and get me back."

"Aww, that's so romantic," Molly awws, a soft expression on her face.

My mouth opens in surprise. Molly is supposed to be on my side with this! She's supposed to be against him doing all of this!

"Molly!" I hiss, "you're supposed to be on my side."

She rolls her brown eyes and sits back in her seat.

"I am, as your best friend I'm supposed to look out for you and make sure your best interests are at heart. This is exactly what I'm doing. Its clear as day he still has feelings for you and I know somewhere in that rock hard heart you have feelings for him too. Plus you two are so meant to be." She explains and gives me a smile.

Stunned at her logic, I fall back into my chair. Do I actually still have such feelings for him? Pff no, of course, I don't.

You're lying to yourself and you know it. My inner subconscious says. Deep down I know I am but I'm only looking out for myself. I need to put on a strong front. I know to prove to myself and others that things like this don't affect me anymore.

"Ava, you do love him. There's a little twinkle in your eyes whenever he's close by or mentioned. I know you're scared of being hurt again and that's completely understandable but you two, you are meant to be. Anyone can tell that there's a connection there, even you. I'm not saying forgive him straight away, all I'm saying is give him a chance."

Molly then opens a blank page in her book and starts doodling. She knows I need to think this through.

The teacher then makes an appearance, five minutes late. He tells us to complete the algebra questions on the sheet below. If there's one thing I hate more than anything else, its freaking algebra. So instead, I decide to think about what Molly said.

Maybe you should give Max a chance, you can obviously see how bad he feels about what you did. My conscious reasons. Its true, Molly even told me that Max has never been the same since that day. He's never approached a girl and hardly interacts with everyone.

I can see the remorse in Max's eyes, the regret is as clear as day. But I'm not going to be guilt—tripped into forgiving him, I am so much stronger than that.

"Molly," I whisper quietly. Molly's head lifts up from the book and gives me a curious look. The class is relatively quiet, most people are reading the book whilst some others are having hushed conversations. Our teacher is on his phone, not being very discreet about it.

"Yes?" She asks.

"D—do you really think I should give him another chance?" I stutter out. Its always good to have someone else's opinion, especially someone who you trust.

Molly frantically nods her head, "definitely. You won't regret it."

I mumble thanks to her and bite my lip. Won't I regret it? I better not.

I can't believe I'm actually going to give Max a second chance.

***

"You are dismissed," our Maths teacher mutters and sits back down at his desk. Once again disregarding us.

I sigh and pack my things up. When I've finished, I link arms with Molly and we both head out of the classroom.

"Sunshine," Max calls out from the hallway. He confidently strolls over to us and gives me a small smile. Some people openly gawk at us, or should I say, Max. I recall Molly telling me how he never properly interacted with girls and this must be a shock for everyone.

"Max," I greet and hug my folders closer to my chest.

"So its lunch and I—I was wondering if you...maybe. .."Max stammers and coughs. "I was wondering if you wanted to go out and get lunch with me."

Now I would have normally instantly declined his offer but then I remember my new promise. Give him a second chance.

With that in mind, I give Max a genuine smile and accept.

"Ava, listen. I know you hate me and all but I would really like to tr--hold on, did you just accept my offer?" Max cautiously asks, having to do a double take. I giggle at him. He really didn't expect me to say yes.

I think I broke Max because his face is gobsmacked.

"You—you just giggled. It was the same laugh you did from two years ago, the one I fell in love with." And to my embarrassment, I blush at his words. Molly nudges me and wiggles her eyebrows.

Ignoring her, I nod. "Yeah, I guess I did."

Max doesn't say anything, he just stands there staring at me with amazement.

I clear my throat before his staring gets too creepy. He looked at me like I was the only girl in the world, that I was the most special thing ever. As sweet as it is, I have to remind myself that it's going to be a long time until I even think about dating him again.

Baby steps.

"So where are you taking me?" I ask Max, knocking him out of his state.

Max gives me that signature smirk from two years ago and speaks, "you'll just have to wait and see."

Playfully rolling my eyes, I start walking out of the school with Max stood right next to me.

13

13 | Ghosts Could Totally Exist

"Hello! And welcome to Cal's Diner, what can I get you two?" An overly cheerful woman greets with a bright smile.

"Uh...can I have burger and fries with a strawberry milkshake please?" Max asks the woman, giving her a small smile.

She beams at him and writes down the order. She then lifts her head up and brushes a bit of her dark brown hair out of the way. "And what can I get you, honey?"

"I'll have the same please," I politely tell her and she nods, walking off to the kitchen.

As soon as she leaves, we are left in silence again. I don't think I can say its a painful and awkward silence because it's not. This type of silence is more comfortable.

Max's brown eyes gaze at me in adoration, once again. I noticed the whole car journey here, he would glance at me. I bet if he wasn't driving, he wouldn't have turned away from my face. I also noted how his hands would twitch on the steering wheel.

Two years ago, whenever we would get a lift from one of our parents or when we would get the bus, Max would be holding my hand. When I questioned him about it, he would claim it was because he feared he would lose me if I wasn't holding his hand. Of course, my heart would thump in my chest and I would blush.

Now, it still happens. A massive part of me feels angry at myself for letting me still feel so affected by him. I tried so hard to get over him yet I'm still feeling like a lovesick fool.

You're giving him a chance. I once again remind myself. Maybe one day, when I finally feel like Max's punishment is up, will I open my heart for him to see. I already have a feeling I'm doing that.

"So Ava, what made you move here? Is it because you missed me?" Max jokes, giving me his trademark smirk. I still can't phantom Bree's words on Max being all closed off after our break up. Max seems so carefree again, well around me at least. Earlier, he wasn't as much but that was because he was trying to 'win me back'.

I roll my eyes at Max, "no. We moved because my dad was offered a better—paid job. This is all a coincidence."

"Or fate." I hear Max mumble under his breath.

"You're still on about that? Feeling superstitious, are we? Tell me, Max, have you seen a ghost yet?" I ask Max whilst trying to refrain myself from smiling.

Max catches onto what I said and grins.

You see, not too long after we started dating, I invited Max round my apartment so that we could watch a movie. He obviously agreed. So there we were watching a film in the dark, with only the TV on. And then we hear a bang and Max ends jumping off of the couch and drops onto the floor. I frowned and asked him what was wrong to which he replied nothing shakily.

He then ran out of the living room and went into the bathroom. I rushed to him and found him searching the bathroom. Eventually, he told me he was searching for a ghost. I nearly laughed, thinking he was joking but when I caught onto his very serious face, I stopped myself. Max told me he has a fear of them, even though he knows they aren't real.

I comforted him and told him that it was alright; that one day, he may actually find evidence of their existence.

"For now though, I will protect you," I had whispered into his ear whilst hugging him. Max's response was to snuggle more with me and bury his head in the crook of my neck.

"Oh, you can bet that I've been keeping watch. I swear, I nearly caught footage of their existence." Max claims, leaning further back into the booth.

"Right..." I drawl out, totally believing him.

The waiter from earlier than brings our food out. The smell hits me like a wave and makes my stomach growl. We both thank her and she heads off.

I waste no time in digging into my food, nearly moaning at how good it tastes.

"This is so good," I moan, closing my eyes. I need to add this diner to my list of places to eat in emergencies.

I open my eyes and look at Max, only to see him staring at me in lust. Honestly, right now Max looks like a man who has been deprived of lust or even...me.

"Ava, please don't make noises like that. It makes me feel..." Max trails off, his brown eyes staring off into the distance.

I give Max a confused look, tilting my head slightly to the side, "what Max? What does it make you feel?"

Max doesn't reply straight away. I nearly repeat my question to him but before I can, he answers. "Desire. Happiness and sadness. Sadness for what I missed, for what I ruined."

Well, I didn't expect that.

Max has always been honest though. Despite my doubts earlier, I know Max is an honest person. When it comes to emotions and feelings, he may be more reluctant to tell me but he will. He will because he knows I appreciate it.

The fact Max feels guilty sends a pang to my heart.

Max isn't the only one who thought about where we could be now. If we were still together, I imagined that right now we would still be going strong, despite our separation. I always imagined we would meet in the holidays; talk on the phone or skype each other every day. I wonder if Max ever thought the same way as me.

"I honestly don't know how to reply to that," I tell Max, eating a chip. Max watches me, drinking in every detail.

"You don't have to. I'm just going to remind you that I want you back. Every second we spend together, I'm going to make you the happiest, I'm going to prove to you that not only do I love you but I am the right man for you. You recall those amazing memories from two years ago? You remember how I always made you laugh or smile? Well, I'm going to continue doing that because I love you and because I want you. I'm not giving up on you Ava." Max says, his voice laced with truthfulness.

My heart is hammering in my chest at his words, at the honesty in his eyes.

How am I supposed to take this whole forgiving process slow when Max gives monologues like that? At this rate, if he continues, I will be melted ice cream in his hands by next month. Maximum.

"Wow," I mutter out, lost for words. "D—do you mean all of that?"

Max bobs his head up and down to confirm it.

"Of course I do, I'm never going to lie or deceive you again. I'm not going to lose you." He explains.

Aww, that is so sweet. I swear, I'm feeling all mushy.

Since Max, I haven't wanted to get into a relationship. Sure, I've gotten drunk at parties and kissed guys and stuff but I have never been back in a relationship. Guys have called me gorgeous, stunning etc but they have never said words like that to me.

Love is hard to find. Its hard to find a decent and honest guy out there in the real world. We girls fantasize about guys, about how they are the perfect people who literally drop to their knees for you but we know that it's very rare that you find somebody like that.

Now that I know the truth about two years ago, I know that Max is a guy who I should fight for. He's one of the decent ones.

"Who knew you could be sentimental?" I tease, smiling at him. I catch Max's brown eyes light up at my smile as he returns it. The very fact that he feels pleased and proud of himself for getting me to smile, warms me to the core.

"Only for you Miss Ava," he teases back, genuinely smiling at me.

Momentarily, I'm stunned by the full beauty of his smile. I blink and then give him a nervous smile. I hope he doesn't notice the effect he has on me—otherwise, I will never hear the end of it.

"Well, if you are bringing formalities into it then I hope you being a gentleman will pay for my food since I didn't bring any money with me," I tell him, faking a posh British accent.

Max grins, "why of course. I hate seeing a damsel in distress."

14

14 | Ava Vs Cheerleaders

"—tomorrow night," I catch the end of Molly's sentence. Everybody—the gang—nod their heads in excitement except for me. Instead, I give them a confused look.

Molly sighs and raises an eyebrow, "were you even listening?"

I shake my head with a smile. "Nope," I say, popping the 'p' just to annoy her.

Molly rolls her eyes. "So we decided that tomorrow we can go to the movies to watch the Incredibles 2!" Molly repeats, squealing.

My mouth makes an 'o' shape. "But its only Wednes day..."

"So?" Bree asks, moving closer to Molly.

"Sure, why not? I literally have nothing better to do with my life," I reply, laughing at how that actually sounds. "Damn, they made me sound like such a loner."

Everybody laughs at that.

"It really did," Josh says.

Luke slings his arm over my shoulder and pushes me closer to him. "Its okay babe, I don't think you're a loner. I will always be here for you."

I try to refrain myself from rolling my eyes at Luke's comment and instead shrug his arm that is casually on my shoulder off. Its like, no matter how many times I tell Luke that I'm not going to get with him, he won't listen. Does it go in one ear and out through another? Does he zone out when I tell him?

Maybe if I record myself saying it and put it on repeat when I'm with him, it will go through his head. Now that could work...

But it sounds a bit too mean. Which is something I'm totally not...

"So tomorrow it is then." Molly reiterates and we all nod our heads.

It's strange, all of this. I met these people yesterday and I already feel like I've known them my whole life. They make me feel at home again, that I belong here. I don't feel like an outsider.

"What's tomorrow?" A deep voice asks from behind me. Instantly, I recognize it. My body reacts to it—goosebumps erupt on my skin and I shiver. It's so unfair how his voice is so attractive and deep. It's so unfair how manly he sounds.

I swivel around to see a smirking Max.

From my peripheral vision, I can see everyone's shocked faces. I mentally curse Max for coming over here, now I'm going to deal with their inquisitive questions. Only Molly knows right now about me accepting Max...as a friend.

"Nothing Max," I tell him with a scowl; his brown eyes flash with amusement. His pink and perfect lips curl upwards into a smirk. The fact that he finds my lack of answer amusing has me feeling unsure.

Its like we are playing a chess game. And right now Max is the one in the lead. The worst part is that he know's he's got a lead.

"Oh really?" He practically taunts, crossing his muscly arms over his broad chest. "Judging by your answer, I think not."

I mentally kick myself for acting like that. Max used to know me better than myself. Apparently, he somewhat still does.

"Its none of your business Max," I say and turn back around to face the rest of the gang in the circle we have formed by Molly's locker.

Ignoring their gazes on either me or Max, I watch a group of cheerleaders at the opposite side of the corridor gossiping about a younger girl.

Before I make a move to go and help her, another arm slings around my shoulder. From the electricity shooting down my arm and spine, I know its not Luke but Max. My heart thumps in my chest and my head begins to go crazy at the proximity.

Goddammit.

"Sweetheart, you are always my business," Max whispers into my ear, his lips brushing against my ear. It takes a lot of restraint to keep myself from wanting to grab his face and smash his lips against mine.

My whole body freezes. Max seems to notice my state and smirks. I so want to hit him on the head or something right now for his cocky behavior. He really does take great pleasure in this.

Is this even what friends do? Because it really doesn't feel like something they would do. I friend zoned Max—sad, I know—so surely we should be acting like friends. This feels intimate, too intimate.

Eventually, I manage to get out of this state and compose myself. Clearing my throat, I knock Max's arm off of my shoulder. "Max, you are invading my personal space, which is something I do not like. I feel violated so please can you take a few steps back."

Max doesn't say anything. He puts his hands up in mock surrender and grins.

My eyes go to the gang who are all staring at us still. Molly has a smirk on her face, Bree has a look of disbelief and the look like they have no idea what to make of this.

"So you friend zoned him too?" Luke asks, incredulously.

"Nah, I just let her believe that mate," Max mutters to him, loud enough for me to hear. I bet he did that on purpose as well.

"Hey!" I protest, "I did friendzone you mate."

"Sure, sure."

I swear to god...

"So, who wants to tell me where you are going tomorrow?" Max asks the whole gang.

"To the cinema." Comes Harry's reply.

I give him a glare, unhappy that he so easily gave it away. Harry only gives me a sheepish look, shrugging his shoulders. Thanks, Harry, thanks.

"Great," Max smiles and claps his hands together. "I love going to the cinema."

"Woah, hold up buddy. Nobody invited you." I assert.

"You didn't have to honey, I invited myself," Max announces, grinning ear to ear. Gosh, does he want a punch in the face because I swear, he is asking for it. Its like he has 'punch me' stamped on his cheek.

"If Max is going, then I'm not going." I declare.

Two can play this game.

Max's face falters for a second but he quickly masks it. It appears I'm the only one who noticed it though.

"Well, if you're not going, I won't either. How about I keep you company instead and let the rest of them go?"

I give Max a glare at the suggestion. "I'm not going because of you!"

"Aww baby, you're hurting my feelings."

My fingers twitch as I try to control my anger. I want to rip my hair out right now or strangle something. Max is doing this on purpose, he's trying to get me to react and prove that he gets to me.

I have a short temper. Anyone who has known me for a while knows I get angry easily. It's not my fault I have a short fuse, I blame it on my mom. Max also knows it. I bet he wants to see me explode to get a kick out of it.

Max always liked to get on my nerves. It was his specialty.

"Ugh fine! You can go!" I yell, lifting my hands up in defeat. Stupid Max.

He grins to himself, his brown eyes lighting up in success. Ugh.

"Damn, the sexual tension between those two is enough to leave me feeling hot and bothered," Bree comments to Molly in a low voice. I send her a scowl to which her lips lift upwards for a second.

"Right so what time tomorrow?" Max asks and I zone out.

My eyes go back to where the three cheerleaders were earlier with the young girl. I now notice that the young girl has pressed herself up against the lockers as all three of the taller cheerleaders surround her.

The frightened face the young girl makes breaks my heart.

I hate bullying. Like so many other people, I despise it. I think people who do it are low. Sure, they probably have problems of their own but to take it out on somebody else who is weaker than you is just plain wrong. It makes me sick to my stomach on how many people do it.

The leader of the group—the girl in the middle who has this aura of order and control—says something to the girl that has her shaking in fear.

Without a second thought, I storm over to them.

Stopping behind them, I tap the middle girl's shoulder. She turns around, wearing a displeased expression.

Briefly, her eyes widen at me but she covers it up. "Yes?"

"Hi! I'm Ava and I'm new here. You must be the schools resident bully, correct?" I ask her in a sickly sweet fake voice. My voice has gone like two octaves higher; has me cringing. Ouch, it hurts my poor ears.

The leader, who has red hair and hazel eyes, frowns. "Uh...yeah?"

I nearly smirk at her confused voice.

"Good. I'm here to warn you to leave this poor girl alone. Bullying is wrong and low. You should feel ashamed of yourself for doing such a low thing. Its—"

"Who do you think you are?" The girl screeches, putting her hands on her bony hips. I wince at her voice.

"Right now I'm your worst nightmare." I give her an innocent smile, flicking my hair off of my shoulder in a sassy way for the hell of it. "Now scram."

Without a second thought, she stumbles away with her posse. Honestly, I thought she would put up more of a fight or would yell at me more but apparently not. Oh well, at least I didn't have to waste any more of my energy on her.

My head turns to the young girl who is shaking in fear. Her petrified face only angers me more. I absolutely hate bullies.

"Hey," I softly say to her hoping to calm her down. "Its okay now, they won't bother you again, I'll make sure of that."

The girl frantically nods her head and rushes off. My eyes stay on her until she slams the main doors open.

I turn back around to the group who either look stunned by my heroism or are in awe. I blank all of that out and wave to them. Home time is my favorite part of the day—actually, I think its everyone's favorite part of the day. Not that I blame them or anything.

And with that, I turn on my heel and march out.

15

15 | Getting Hitched

"Cali sucks without you honey, it totally sucks." My best friend comments. I'm currently lying on my comfy bed with my books surrounding me and my headphones in so that I can talk to Rosie, my very good friend who I 'abandoned'.

"Aww," I say, "I'm flattered. Honestly, it's so sweet to hear that. I guess you weren't exaggerating when you said you couldn't last a week without me."

I hear Rosie huff on the other side of the phone which makes me smirk. I just love to tease this girl.

"You know what? I'm retracting that. I'm unsaying it and pinning on the 'that never happened board'". Rosie replies in an overdramatic voice. I swear to god this girl is the queen of drama. She's so melodramatic, all of the freaking time.

And that's why she's my best friend.

"Anyways, how is LA? The place where you either get hitched or go into debt." Rosie asks me.

I roll my eyes at her statement. Does she really think I'm going to either get married or gamble away all of my parent's money? I mean, I might gamble away some money if it goes to a good cause—like my stomach—but otherwise, I won't.

"Right, firstly, I'm not old enough to get hitched. Secondly, I'm not even in the city! I'm practically in a small town on the outskirts of LA where nothing happens. Well, saying that— you know what? Nevermind." I ramble. My fingers are fiddling with my pen, a habit I do all of the time. My fingers just have to be doing something.

"I'm sorry, did you finish? I just got really tired there," Rosie then adds to her 'tiredness' by yawning, loudly.

"Hey!" I protest, "I was only telling you the truth."

"But the truth sounds so boring." Rosie whines in her four — year — old voice. "I prefer the image I have in my head. Right now I'm imagining you in a fancy house that has a view of the flashing lights and the drunk people."

Once again, I roll my eyes at Rosie's description. Of course, I had to be best friends with the most over imaginative person ever. I'm not complaining or anything but sometimes she really manages to blow me away with her weirdness. I love her to death, don't get me wrong but she seriously manages to astound me on numerous occasions.

I guess that's why Rosie is great in art and story writing. Our meeting was very coincidental. We are two completely different people, with different aspirations and hobbies.

We met before everything happened with Max. It was freshman year and Rosie had moved to our school. At the time, I had no knowledge about this at all. We accidentally bumped into each other in the lunch hall and spilled our trays on each other.

Back then, I was more reserved. I wasn't the outgoing Ava today, I was quiet. I guess you can thank Max for that.

Anyways, she yelled at me for being clumsy whilst I repeatedly apologized to her. After letting her frustrations out on me, we both cleaned the mess we made and went to the bathrooms. She introduced herself as did I and we just bonded from there. One could say we became friends because we were so different that we just bounced off of each other.

Rosie was more confident than me, she was flirty and a party animal. I was quiet and liked to blend in with the crowds.

And then Max happened. After I left the hotel and came home, Rosie was the first person I called. I told her everything, from the last night we spent together to the horrific morning. She came to my house thirty minutes later with three speeding tickets and a tub of my favorite ice cream—Ben and Jerry's.

I sobbed on her shoulder the whole night about it, retelling my tragic break up story. Rosie helped me through my healing process—something that I will always be grateful for.

Five weeks later, I officially became the new and improved Ava. I ditched my shyness, I escaped my darkroom and became wild. I partied hard, hooked up with guys and spoke back to any person who insulted me.

Rosie was beside me the whole time, guiding me. She made sure I never went too extreme, that I never assaulted a popular person when I got into a fight with them. She backed me up every time and helped me block Max out.

And ever since then, she's been my right—hand woman at parties and school. We were basically the A—team. But with only two members.

"Rosie, please can you get your head out of the gutter?"

I hear Rosie huff on the other side of the line and I can imagine her rolling her grey eyes.

"Fine, fine." She says, sounding rather reluctant to stop messing with me. It's her main trait—she loves teasing people. If we were a superhero group, she would be the comic relief. "So, did you make any friends? Specifically a good friend?"

Is that jealousy I detect in her voice? Hm...

"Why yes, yes I did." I truthfully answer, thinking of my new brown and ginger—haired girlfriends. I suppose the three boys count as good friends as well, they seem nice. Even Luke, the biggest flirt in the world who doesn't understand me. I bet if I hit him with a sign saying 'not interested' he would blank it out and continue to pursue me.

"Ooh, what are they like?" She asks in a curious and interested voice. If there's one thing I'm certain about Rosie, its that she is always interested in every aspect of her friend's lives. It shows she cares about me; that she is a true friend but even when I don't really want to tell her anything, I end up doing it.

If I tried to lie to her, Rosie would always know. She is a human lie detector.

"They are nice. There's Molly who is the nicest person ever. She's shy, a bit like me in freshman year. She's super pretty as well, I'm actually really envious of her. And then there's Bree, she's a real spitfire. She even has firey red hair. They are great people; I know you would definitely like them." I tell Rosie.

Rosie hums. I hear rustling on her side of the phone meaning she's moving around. Patiently, I wait for Rosie to stop moving around. So I zone out and think about food and what I'm going to watch on Netflix when I've finished my dreaded homework.

A thump and a yelp from Rosie has me coming back to reality. She curses under her breath, not loud enough for me to hear, unfortunately. Rosie has a sailor's mouth.

"You okay there?" I gently ask her when I don't hear any noise.

For a moment, I don't get a reply. I begin to think maybe she cut the call or the connection died but I'm proven wrong when I hear Rosie's breathless voice.

"I'm here and I'm okay. I think. Just had a bit of an...accident. That's all."

"Right..." I drawl out, not entirely convinced.

"Right so, where were we?" Rosie questions and I nearly facepalm.

"We were discussing my new friends," I inform her.

"Ah yes, the friends who are replacing me," she adds confidently yet I can hear the sadness in her voice. I feel a pang in my heart. I hate that my friend is doubting our friendship.

"Rosie," I start in a soft voice," you know that they will never replace you. You are my best friend. Always. I mean, do you really think binge—watching TV shows will be the same with them? Do you honestly think we will obsess over characters from Stranger Things and The Originals in the same way? No, the answer is no. You are my best friend. You know me better than anyone."

"Yeah, yeah. I know. I'm sorry for thinking you will forget about me...its just...school isn't the same without you. I'm having withdrawal symptoms. I'm sorry, I trust you. Always." She sighs out, relieved. Rosie just needed some reassurance that I wouldn't abandon her.

"Rosie, can—can I get your advice on something?" I nervously ask her, suddenly realizing I didn't tell my best friend that I saw my arch nemesis, the devil himself. Max.

Rosie responds instantly, "of course. Ask away."

Swallowing, I try to find a way to word it. How do I tell her that I not only saw my ex-boyfriend who cheated on me but that I also friend zoned him? She was there when I cried my eyes out until they were sore when I holed myself in my room and refused to leave.

She saw how badly it affected me. She saw how broken I became.

I honestly don't think Rosie will be the same as Molly, all because she was there to see how damaged I was. Sure, I told Molly the best I could that it messed me up badly but she didn't see how heartbroken I was.

"Uh...well...you see, I sorta saw Max, you know Max?" Max, the one who broke my heart and left me with trust issues. Yeah, him. "Anyways, I saw him and he kind of locked me in the janitors closet and explained to me what happened two years ago and I sort of told him that I would give him a chance. So we are like friends now." I rush out, squeezing my eyes shut as I wait for Rosie to explode with questions.

However, that doesn't happen. She doesn't say anything. The silence is deafening, absolutely horrible. I can clearly hear all of the quiet background noise here, in my room and wherever Rosie is.

I don't know if I prefer no response or Rosie bursting out with questions.

"Rosie?" I cautiously whisper, dropping the pen in my hand so that I can drag my hand through my thick hair.

"Yeah? Sorry, I was just...lost in thought. My head was just processing the bullshit I heard." Rosie remarks in a strong and rather irritated voice.

"Rosie—"

"No!" She interjects. "Max is a dick, he's scum. He broke your heart. He shattered it and left you to clear it up. He doesn't deserve your forgiveness. Hell, he doesn't even deserve to breathe the same air as you."

A lump forms at the back of my throat at her words. I knew she wouldn't agree with my choice but I didn't expect her to say such words.

Maybe I did make the wrong choice. Maybe I should have made Max suffer for longer. But, it was my choice.

"Rosie, listen to—"

"I swear Ava, do I need to bash your head against my locker? Max isn't good for you, you should stay completely away from him. Ignore his existence!" She shrieks, not stopping her rambling. "I just don't get—"

"Please listen to me," I beg her.

"—why you would do that." She continues.

I let out a defeated sigh. How am I supposed to get through to her? Why won't she shut her gob for five seconds?

"Rosie, you may not understand why I did it but believe me when I say I wanted to. It's my choice. Not yours, not Max's, mine. So, as a good friend, I hope you understand why and accept it." I slowly say, biting my lip after finishing.

"I'm sorry Ava but I just can't right now. When he breaks your heart, don't come calling me." She says with a disappointed tone and hangs up.

I sit there, staring at my phone in disbelief and...betr ayal. My eyes sting slightly but I'm quick to rub them.

You will not cry, I coach myself.

I...I just can't believe she would do that to me. Just.. .leave me there without any support.

In anger, I chuck my phone against the wall and grab my pillow. Quickly, I stuff my face in it and scream. I don't know where this anger, frustration came from. But I do know that letting it out feels good, more uplifting.

16

16 | Silly Games

After what happened with Rosie, I tried to finish my homework. However, I just couldn't concentrate. Rosie's words echoed in my head on repeat. I can't believe she would hang up like that. I understand she's mad, I really do. But I thought as a supportive friend, she would be there for me.

After many hours of zoning in and out of my homework, I managed to complete it. I decided I would try and call Rosie now. I'm hoping she's calmed down from earlier on and will be more reasonable to talk to.

With that in mind, I stumble over to where I chucked my phone and dial her number. Luckily my phone didn't smash when I threw it in anger. The phone rings for a few seconds until it suddenly cuts off.

Frowning, I pull the phone away and see that she's declined my call. Great.

I try again but once again, my attempts are left nothing successful. Clearly, Rosie is being stubborn. She won't answer the phone until she thinks I will have come to my senses. It could be days or weeks before she answers my calls again.

Sighing at that thought, I dump my phone on my bed and turn my tablet on. Netflix will cure me.

***

"Hello!" Molly happily chirps when I see her by my locker. Bree is stood next to her with her things already.

"Hi," I mumble unpleasantly and pull my locker open. The whole night I tossed and turned with me and Rosie's argument invading my thoughts. I couldn't sleep a wink because of it. And when I don't get a good amount of sleep, I'm moody as hell. Literally, I'm a groggy mess who you don't want to be around.

"Woah, what's got you all cranky this morning?" Bree asks, taken back by my very unhappy state.

"Friend. Phone. Max. Sleep." I reply, rather incoherently. My brain is a jumbled up mess of everything. The fact that I have to go to lessons is not something I want.

They both give me confused looks but I don't choose to elaborate. Heaving my heavy bag in my locker, I get my books out and slam the locker shut. Both of the girls jump back in fright at it.

"Are you okay Ava? You seem rather..." Molly trails off. She seems unsure of how to describe my current mood. In fact, I suspect she's scared of my reaction to what I say. In this state, I'm rather unpredictable. I don't even know how I would react.

"Not really," I truthfully answer and turn my back to my locker so I can lean against it. Tiredly, I run my free hand down my face whilst my other hand holds my two books for the next couple of hours. "And you can say whatever you wanted to say. I won't go berserk on you, I promise."

Molly sighs and then finishes her sentence. "Temperamental."

"Do you want to tell us about it?" Bree asks me softly, placing her pale hand on my arm for comfort. I give her a small smile at the warm gesture. Little does she know, knowing someone is there to back you up and listen is a big thing for me.

"I told my best friend from Cali that I saw Max again and that I befriended him. She got mad because she's rather protective of me so we got into a massive fight. Before I could explain myself anymore, she hung up on me. And now she's refusing to answer my calls." I rush out so quickly my mind can't even keep up with what I'm saying.

"Oh," comes from Bree.

"I'm sorry Ava." Molly sympathetically says, "I'm sure everything will work out in the end."

That's what I'm hoping for.

The bell rings and we quickly walk to our separate lessons. I nearly groan when I step into the loud English literature classroom. If there's one thing my head can never comprhened, its old texts like Shakespeare. I get that he's an important part of the world and that he did something truly magnificent but teaching it to teenagers who just don't care really isn't a good idea.

The only reason I revise it is because I want to get into a good university. Having a good grade from English literature under my belt will help me.

Sitting down on a desk in the middle of the class-room, I open up my book. This is my second time in this class and from what I've gathered from my teacher, he's a little too enthusiastic for this subject. Not that its a problem but, for a bunch of seniors, it's not the best.

"Okay class, let's begin today's lesson shall we?" He asks whilst dumping his bag on his desk. "Can you open your books to page—"

Mr. Andrews, our teacher, is cut off by a loud bang. Every head in this classroom snaps towards the door. Standing there, with a cocky smirk on his handsome face is Max. He strolls in, blanking out the gawking eyes from the girls and gives our teacher a small apology for being late.

Mr. Andrews rolls his eyes and mutters something under his breath. With an annoyed sigh, he orders Max to find a seat. I didn't know Max was in this class. He must have bunked the previous lesson I was in.

Max's eyes scan the classroom and stop when they see me. With a grin, he confidently heads over to the empty seat beside me. I cuss myself for choosing a desk that wasn't surrounded by people.

I keep my head facing forward and listen to Mr. Andrew's instructions. When he has given out the task to do, he sits down in front of his desk and starts marking. That's everyone's cue to begin talking.

From my peripheral vision, I see Max swivel around in his chair to completely face me.

"Psst, Ava," Max whispers and pokes me. Yes, pokes me.

I ignore Max and start my Macbeth work. Explain, using subject terminology and quotes from the play, how Shakespeare portrays Macbeth's madness.

I groan at the question and run a hand through my hair. Why does Shakespeare have to be so hard to understand?

"Yo Ava." An annoying voice prods again.

Just ignore him. Just ignore him. Pretend he's a figurement of your imagination. I chant in my head over and over. Friend or not, I am in no mood to talk to him again. I just want to get this day over and done with.

"Did you know ignoring your friend isn't very nice. You're not making a good impression." Max remarks.

Don't reply. He's trying to wind you up. Its an old trick of Max's.

Out of nowhere, Max knocks the back of my head, hard. I flinch forwards from the action and throw a glare his way. I rub the now stinging bit of my head with an irritated expression on my face. The asshole!

"What the hell Max?" I ask him with a scowl.

Max only smirks at my reaction. "You wouldn't answer so I had to find another way to get your attention."

"Well, you don't hit your friends head." I scold him. "It's not nice."

"Sunshine, you shouldn't have ignored me then," Max replies, using the nickname he used to call me. I feel a sad pang in my heart at it.

I send Max another scowl.

"You have my attention now so what do you want?" I begrudgingly ask him.

"Well, since I'm on a mission to find my sunshine, I think we need to play a small game." He announces, his brown eyes sparkling.

I've never seen Max so hyped by the prospect of a game. He really does look excited to do this.

I nearly forgot about the whole 'finding Ava' mission he created. The whole friend's ordeal has blocked any of those thoughts. Now that he's brought it back up, I'm curious as to what he has planned. If he thinks he's going to find that shy and naive girl, he's wrong. Not even I know where she's gone.

"This is a lesson, Max. That means we have to do work." I emphasize 'work' so that he gets it through his head that I want to get this done today. I already have quite a bit of homework—which is crazy as its only my third day! You'd think teachers would be nice but apparently not.

Max shrugs and waves it off. "Who cares? This is more important."

Well, I'm glad to see one of us cares about our education.

"Max, can you not do this later? Like at lunch?" I suggest. If I were to play this game, I would rather play it at lunch when I don't have work to do.

"I'd prefer playing it now because I have your attention and its just us too." He replies and winks at the 'just us' part.

"Seriously?" I ask, raising an eyebrow.

Max nods his head and shuffles in his seat to get comfortable.

"Right so the game is simple. I will ask you a question about me and you will answer what you think is right. Its based on the knowledge we had of each other two years—"

"Hold up," I interrupt him. "Just to clarify, you are doing this see if we've changed since two years ago?"

"Ding ding." He says loudly. I give him an unimpressed look.

"Do you need an example?"

"Uh..." comes my unsure reply.

Max clears his throat. "So, you ask me what I think your favorite film is and I will say The Notebook because that's what it was two years ago. If I'm wrong, you will correct me."

That makes sense I guess.

"But I still don't understand how that is going to find the old me." I reiterate my thoughts.

Max gives me a smirk. "It will show me and you how much you've changed. Plus, it will bring back memories. I think you've misinterpreted the 'finding Ava' thing. I know I will never completely get the old you back. And I don't want to do that. I know you've grown stronger since that day. I don't want you to forget about everything, you shouldn't. What I mean by me trying to find Ava is that I'm trying to show you who you've become. You are more stubborn, more confident and headstrong. I don't want to change you, I only want to show you how strong you've become. You don't realize it but you are inspirational and amazing. I am so fucking proud of you."

I'm left gobsmacked by Max's words. My jaw has completely unhinged from my body and my eyes are practically bugging out of its sockets. I have never been complimented so much.

The purpose of this is to show me how strong I've become. I know I'm stronger now, I've built walls around my heart to protect it. But me inspirational? Pfft, please. I'm not exactly Gandhi.

I'm also baffled by how wise Max is now. He sounds so much mature than what he was two years ago. Perhaps if he's accomplished his mission, I will tell him. We've both changed—for the better.

Before I can input any of my thoughts, Max is clearing his throat. "And now we can play the game."

17

17 | Broccoli Is Just Bleh

"First question," Max starts, eagerly leaning closer to me. "What is my least favorite vegetable?"

Easy question. I recall our second date very well. Max took me to a small restaurant in the city and ordered a roast dinner. As soon as he saw what was in the dish, he went crazy. He complained to our poor waiter for ten minutes that he brought that disgusting and abysmal thing to him. I remember trying to cover my giggles with coughs because it was so bizarre. I mean, he was acting irrationally. It was excessive to act like that for a bit of broccoli but I didn't mind. It was the high light of my day.

Personally, now that I remember, I think he acted like that on purpose just to make me laugh. The sly looks he gave me when I was having 'coughing' fits was a clear indicator that he actually just wanted to get me laughing.

Oh, Max.

"Broccoli," I confidently reply, smirking.

Max cockily raises his eyebrow, the ends of his lips tugging upwards. "You sure?"

I roll my eyes in annoyance. "Yes, I'm sure. Stop trying to make me doubt myself."

Max holds his arms up in mock surrender. "Woah, sunshine. I didn't do anything. You're the one jumping to conclusions here."

I give Max a cold glare and purse my lips. Stupid Max. Once again he's teasing me. I swear, this boy is going to be the death of me with all of his teasing.

"I'm positive Max."

Max leaves another dramatic pause, trying to make suspense. Or perhaps its just to aggravate me even more. I bet its the latter.

Much to my irritation, it's working as well.

I've always been short tempered. A lovely trait that I inherited from my father. We both get mad at simple things; explode. And when I say explode, we do. Except I don't have steam coming out of my ears. As comical as that is, I don't get that angry.

"Congratulations Sunshine, you're right," Max gives me a breathtaking smile and claps his hands together. "That...I can't even call it food because it's too offensive. Its just so...so bleh."

"Right," I give him an unsure nod. "What's my favorite fast food place?"

There's a pregnant pause between the two of us as Max thoroughly thinks through this. I feel like I can see the wheels turning in his head. His brown eyes will occasionally flicker up to my eyes and he would look like he has an answer but then he would look away and shake his head. Like he was mentally shaking his head.

I must admit, Max does look very cute. Childlike.

"McDonald's!" He exclaims. "You're favorite fast food place is McDonald's because you're obsessed with the chicken nuggets."

Internally, I smile. He remembered. He even remembered the chicken nuggets fact. I'm touched, very touched indeed.

"Yup," I say, popping the 'p'. "I'm actually surprised. Not going to lie."

Max fake gasps and places a hand on his heart. He puckers his lip out and gives me sad puppy eyes. "I. Am. Hurt. Of course, I would remember. You wound me Sunshine."

I can't help it but I end up in a laughing fit. His face, his voice...it was so dramatic and funny. I have to lift my head up to stop the water that's welling up in my eyes to fall down my cheeks.

"Sssh," an angry voice hisses from somewhere close to me. I don't pay any attention though, I'm still too busy dying of laughter.

After a few more minutes, I calm down slightly. My breaths are ragged and my cheeks feel flushed from laughing so hard. From my peripheral vision, I can see Max studying me with his chocolate brown eyes.

He's staring at me like I'm a broken puzzle that's missing a piece. A piece he wants to find.

"Your laugh sounds better than an angel's voice," he comments quietly when I've completely settled down. He sounds distant. I assume it because he's zoning out and is subconsciously saying it.

My head snaps to face him and my cheeks burn bright pink. Again. I have been complimented by many guys before but when it comes from Max, it feels so real and true. There isn't an inkling of dishonesty in his voice. He truly does believe it.

"Thanks, Max."

"Anytime." He mumbles and then jumps back into this reality. Max clears his throat loudly, grabbing the attention of some irritated students nearby who give us stinky looks. One glare from Max though and they are swiveling back around and pretending that it never happened. "Right so, true or false, I have a small scar on my knee from falling off of the swings in fourth grade."

False. It has to be false. I recall Max telling me he once got a scar from falling off of the monkey bars. He said it terrified him; to this day, he won't go anywhere near them just in case he falls off of them again. Despite the fact that he is tall enough to reach the floor now.

"False, you told me this story once on the beach. I remember the day really well now, we were walking by the rocks and I slipped and nearly fell into the sea but you caught me. I had a cut on my foot from scraping it against the rocks and you told me it would scar. To cheer me up, you told me that story. It distracted me from the pain."

We both fall into a silence again. I guess Max is thinking about that day too. That was the day I kissed him for the first time. I can still feel the way his soft, pink lips pressed against mine gently as he poured his emotions onto me.

At that time, we weren't in love. No, but we were close. After that day, I discovered how much I liked Max and how much I wanted to be with him. It scared me to death—I never liked anyone so much before him. Sure, I had pathetic crushes but that's all they were, little crushes that would never happen.

With Max, it could have been something more. Something so much more powerful.

"That was a good day," Max muses, a hint of sadness laced in his voice. His beautiful face frowns as he stares straight ahead of him.

Before I can utter another word or can ask Max a question, the shrilly bell rings. Immediately, students stand up and file out of the classroom. I collect my folder and notepad and walk out. Max follows closely behind me.

The hallways are packed as I walk through them to my next lesson. Students barge into me, none of them looking back to apologize for it. Not that I expected them to though, most teenagers these days don't care about manners.

Wordlessly, Max stands beside me. I note how girls stare at him with lust and desire. Some even try to approach him but he blanks every single one of them. His eyes only ever look at me or the path ahead. He doesn't even glance at them.

My heart thumps faster in my chest at that. It makes me feel glad that he doesn't care. It also proves to me that he is trying to make amends.

When we get to my Economics class, we both come to a halt. Max stands in front of me, close enough that I can faintly see a few freckles to the side of his face but not close enough that my boobs are pressed into his chest.

Apparently, Max doesn't like the distance between us because he moves closer to me, hesitantly. His eyes remain in contact with mine, searching for me to tell him to stop moving closer. I give him no indication to stop.

Now, he's a few inches from me. This time, I can feel his minty breath on my face as he stares down at me.

My breath hitches as he raises a hand to my face and brushes a strand of my brown hair behind my ear.

My heart is hammering inside of my chest in anticipation. Is he going to kiss me? Hug me? Wish me goodbye? WHAT IS HE GOING TO DO?!

When Max slowly leans down towards me, I flutter my eyes closed. My lips part and I clutch the books I'm hugging closer to my chest.

My eyes snap open though when he kisses my cheek. I honestly expected him to kiss me but then again, I told him I didn't want to rush into this.

His lips tingle on my skin and have me shivering, not from the cold. They linger on my cheek for a few glorious seconds and then he's pulling away. I stare at him through my long lashes and chew on my lip.

His eyes watch my lip and narrow. Hastily, he steps back and smiles.

"Have a good lesson. I'll pick you up when its over." He wishes and then goes. I stand there dumbfounded, trying to contemplate what just happened. One minute he was here, staring at my lips and then he was gone.

I blink a couple of times and spin on my heel to go into my classroom.

That was definitely weird.

18

18 | Unicorns Could Exist

Have you ever wanted to know what goes on in someone's head? Like, have you wanted the ability to read minds?

Because right now, I really want to know what's going on in Max's head. He's been staring at me for the past few minutes, deep in thought. Every once in a while, he would frown and shake his head. Like he was shaking his thoughts away.

I've tried making eye contact with him a few times to get his attention but he seems really focused on the table. I know for a fact he's not interested in the boring table, so he's zoned out.

Molly is sat next to me on the lunch table, with Bree to the other side of me. Max, who decided to sit with us today, is opposite me. Lawrence has disappeared to god knows where. According to Molly, he's been pining over some girl for a while now. So he's chasing her down. Lucky girl...

Luke has been good so far. He's refrained himself from making a comment about my appearance or dating. I have a feeling it because Max is here.

Harry is having a deep conversation with Bree. Josh is staring at the two of them intensely. His face is expressionless but his eyes are burning with fury. Whenever Harry makes eye contact with him, he receives a frosty glare. It's such a cold look I have shivers running down my spine. And it wasn't even directed at me!

"Ava?" Molly asks me, snapping out of my thoughts. I glance at her and raise an eyebrow.

"Yes?"

"We're still on for the cinema tonight right?" Instantly, I'm nodding. I'm actually excited to see the film now, partly because Max is coming.

The last time I went to the movies with Max was when we went to see Fast and Furious 7. I remember crying after we left the cinema because of the emotional tribute they gave Paul Walker. Max held onto me whilst I cried into his t-shirt. When I finished crying, he took me to an ice cream parlor to cheer me up.

Max spent the whole time there cracking jokes.

"I'll pick you up—"

"Don't worry, I'll pick her up," Max cuts Molly off. She glances at me and raises an eyebrow. I avert my eyes from her suspicious gaze and stare at Max.

"What were you thinking about?" I blurt out before my mind can even over think the question. The thing about me is I say things before I think them. If I'm curious about something, I will straight up ask it. No thinking.

Max gives me a flattering smirk, "why do you want to know? Jealous I might be thinking about another girl?"

I scowl at Max, hating the fact that I would be very jealous if he was thinking about another girl. Especially since he locked me in the janitors closet and gave me a massive speech about how he wants me back.

"No," I immediately answer and cross my arms over my chest. "I'm just being curious. Is that a crime now?"

Max shakes his head, "you were being nosy."

I gasp and place a hand over my heart, "I was not! Can't a friend just be concerned."

Max winces at the word friend like its the worst word ever. I mean, he should know I wouldn't jump straight back into a relationship. First, he has to pass the test of being my friend. Then he can think about dating me again.

"Aww, you're concerned about me Sunshine. How endearing." Max says in a sickly sweet voice. He's pretending not to be affected by the fact we are friends but I can see the sadness and want glistening in his brown eyes.

He forgets that I know him too.

I roll my eyes and huff. It's clear I'm not going to get an answer from him. I guess I was being a bit nosy but in my defense, he was sitting like that for a while. I was worried. Even if I'm slowly starting to like him, I care for him.

Oh, who am I kidding? I've always cared about Max. Even after the betrayal. I passionately hated him. Max just weaved his way into my heart and snuggled up in a spot there.

"So what time are you planning to pick me up?" I change the subject.

Max gives me a surprised look. He must have thought I would put up a fuss about getting a ride with him. Not anymore.

"Be ready for six thirty." He tells me and I nod.

The bell then rings loudly, signaling the end of lunch. I groan and rub the side of my face. I have P.E. next. Great.

"I'll see you later Sunshine," Max says and smirks when I give him an annoyed look. That nickname...It has my heart thumping in my chest.

***

"Do you think unicorns exist?" Bree asks me as soon as we get into the girls changing rooms. I give her a bewildering look. That was not what I was expecting her to say. One minute I'm talking to her about how much we hate P.E. and now she's randomly asking me this.

That's one adjective to describe Bree. Random.

"Uh," I unsurely drawl out. "Sure. If you want them to be then why not."

Bree shrugs her shoulders and begins to get changed. When we've finished, we both head out into the large sports hall. Our gym teacher is already standing there, waiting. He has an impatient look on his face as he taps his foot on the floor. The last time I met him, he seemed really friendly and nice but today, he looks done with the world.

His blue eyes look really tired. I feel sorry for the guy. Being a teacher must be hard, especially if you are teaching teenagers.

When we all arrive, he clears his throat loudly to get all of our attention.

"So I have some important paperwork to go through today so I'd like you to do some circuit training. I don't care what activities you do, as long as you are doing something. Got it?" He asks, wordlessly, we all nod. With a sigh, he trudges off to his office and shuts the door.

What a great gym teacher. I think sarcastically.

"Sometimes, I absolutely love Mr. James." Bree comments. It's only my second lesson with him and I've gathered that he doesn't really care about P.E.

At least somebody knows that not everyone cares about sport.

"You know what, I'm going to sit on the bleachers. My legs are killing me," Bree tells me and walks over there.

Lawrence is chatting to some rather buff looking guys, laughing with them. He seems busy and engaged in their conversation so I decided to follow Bree.

"Tell me, Bree, how are your legs hurting? You've been sat down all day." I ask her from behind her as I trail after her.

Bree plonks herself on the seat and rests her legs on the bench in front of her.

"I'll have you know walking isn't exactly my specialty. My legs get hurt really easily." She admits. I raise an eyebrow at her in disbelief. She's hardly done any walking. "What can I say? It's not my thing."

I roll my eyes but don't comment back. This girl is worse than me. And I hate doing exercise.

"You know, when he looks at you, its like he's looking at the most precious thing in the world." Bree randomly says. I sit down next to her and give her a perplexed look.

"Huh?"

Bree stares at me for a few seconds like she's trying to figure me out. "You don't know?" She frowns and mutters something to herself that I can't hear.

"Don't know what?" I repeat my full attention on her now. What is it I don't see?

"Max. You don't know how much that guy loves you? It's easy to see! Jeez, even my grandma could see and she's batshit crazy." Bree yells, attracting the attention of some students nearby. With an icy glare from her blue eyes, they scatter away and pretend nothing happened.

Probably a good idea.

"Bree, you're exaggerating. I know he likes me but he doesn't gaze at me like that," I tell her, my voice quivering at the thought of him loving me like I'm the only girl in the world.

Bree huffs annoyed and rolls her shoulders. She then swivels around her seat quickly to face me and lifts a hand up to my head. Before I can question her, she's knocking the side of my head hard.

I flinch, the left side of my head throbbing slightly in pain. I move my head away from her hand but she only continues.

"What are you doing Bree? That hu—ouch!" I yelp and smack her pale arm away. My eyes narrow annoyed at her. "What the hell?" I hiss and massage the place she kept hitting.

"I was trying to knock some sense into you. Have you been losing brain cells recently or are you in cloud cuckoo land?" She asks, inspecting my face again. This girl.

"Not funny," I deadpanned. "Now tell me, what is going on between you and Harry?"

I smirk slyly when Bree quickly turns away from me and runs a hand through her hair.

"Nothing's going on," she mumbles. I nearly scoff.

"Sure, sure."

"There's isn't anything going on. I don't even like him! So SHUT UP!" Bree suddenly bursts out, her eyes blazing. I jump at her sudden mood change and give her a cautious look.

Where did that come from?

"Uh, Bree? I never said you liked him." I mention. She flickers her eyes to me and I swear I see regret her eyes but then it's gone. She stands up and without uttering another word, she's off.

Something is definitely going on with her and I'm going to find out.

Word count: 1750

Sorry for the earlier/late update (depending if you thought I would update yesterday). I was on holid ay...

Anyways, what do you think? Thoughts on Bree????

I might be able to update tomorrow too! Hehe. But don't hold me to that because I get my exam results. Eek!!

Until whenever, bye!!!!

19

19 | Lunge

Chasing Pavements - Adele

19 | Lunge

***

"That was awesome!" Molly exclaims once we come out of the movie theatre. I nod my head in agreement. The film was great.

"You are such a child Molly Wolly," Josh nudges his shoulder with hers. Molly turns to face him with a glare on his face - obviously very annoyed by the nickname he's given her.

"Don't say that again," Molly hisses angrily. Her brown eyes are narrowed like slits, completely focused on Josh.

Josh lifts his hands up in mock surrender. "Sorry, sorry. Jeez, not need to start PMSing on me."

Oh, that did it.

Molly lunges at her brother like a rabid animal. She gives a war cry and jumps on his back. He yelps in shock when she hits him on the back of the head - hard. I burst out in laughter at Josh's stunned and traumatic face.

I guess you should never mess with Molly.

A security guard comes racing through the hall, heading straight towards us. Well, towards Molly and Josh.

"What do you think you're doing?" He asks, harshly. The siblings stop fighting and stare at the man. When they don't answer, he repeats his question.

Molly hops off of Josh's back when she snaps out of her state of shock and blushes. "I-I," she stutters, looking down at the ground whilst fiddling with her fingers. Ferocious Molly is now gone; we're back with shy, kind Molly.

"Just leave," he commands and without a second thought, we all comply. Even I got shivers from that guy. The way he glared at all of us was just chilling.

As soon as we make it out of the theatre, Josh starts scolding Molly for acting barbarically. I turn away. Hearing their argument is not only boring but personal. Instead, I head over to Bree who is teasing Luke. When Bree notices me, her face turns more serious. I almost frown at her sudden change of mood. Did I do something wrong?

"Hey Bree," I start, smiling. "Can I talk to you?"

Her green eyes dart to Molly and Josh who are arguing, then to Lawrence, Harry, and Max who are talking and finally, back to me. Yeah, Max ended up coming to the cinema. He even picked me up, despite my protests.

Admittedly, I enjoyed the ride. We mindlessly chatted about normal things like we were old friends.

There was no awkwardness between us. Everything was comforting. Occasionally, Max would make a comment that would hint towards a relationship but I would brush it off. He knows I'm nowhere near ready to get back into a relationship, especially not with him yet.

"Sure," comes Bree's reply.

I grab her arm and lead her to a more secluded part of the car park. Whilst walking, I feel his eyes on me. I don't need to turn around to see Max - my body already knows it's him.

"Bree, what's going on with you?" I ask her. Her eyes widen at my bluntness; her mouth opens but I cut her off from talking yet. I haven't finished yet, I don't want to hear her say 'what do you mean? Nothing's going on.' "Earlier, you scampered off like your pants were on fire. You overreacted over a simple question and then bit my ear off when I asked you about it."

"I know," she sighs and leans against a car by her. "I'm sorry for acting so strangely. I just don't want anyone to find out."

I give her a confused look. What doesn't she want me to find out? Did something happen between Harry and her? It has to have something to do with him because that's when she reacted berserk.

"What don't you want me to find out?" I ask her softly.

"I didn't want you to find out that Harry and I dated," she answers and I knit my eyebrows together. They dated?

Holy macaroni! That's why she acted so hostile when I first saw them together and why she reacted crazily earlier. She was afraid. Obviously, they had a bad break up.

I am so shocked right now. Harry is the sweet one in the group. I honestly thought he was the only one in the group who hadn't dated. He's so shy and kind.

But him...with Bree? I did not see that happening. Bree and Harry are so different - like polar opposites. Bree is more outgoing, firey whilst Harry is shy. One's an extrovert and the other is an introvert.

"W-why would you be scared? None of us would judge you." I stammer. Bree sighs again and crosses her arms over her chest. She starts rubbing her arms as if she is feeling uncomfortable right now.

"Its embarrassing," she admits. Embarrassing? I don't understand how that would feel embarrassing. Did anyone know about it or something?

I cock my head to the side, trying to figure her out right now. Whilst her body language portrays unease, her eyes are closed off - cold. Its almost as if she is bottling her heart right now, locking it up and throwing away the key.

Bree huffs and elaborates, "I thought I loved him. I really did. We dated for four months, in secret. But when he suggested going public, I freaked. I'm scared, so scared of what people would think, despite always giving off an 'I don't give a fuck' look. But yeah, he got mad and well, we started fighting a lot. One night, the fight got so bad that words that I didn't mean were spoken and we broke up. Ever since then, I've not only regretted everything but

I've been embarrassed. I want to approach him but I don't think he will let me."

For a few seconds, I'm speechless. I'm not entirely sure how to react to what she said. Her situation almost reminds me of Max - not in the cheating way or anything but in a hurt way, the afraid way. We're both hurting but for different reasons. For Bree, she wants Harry back but she's afraid of getting rejected. She doesn't want to be humiliated or told she's not wanted.

Me? I'm afraid of my heart being broken again.

"Bree," I call, capturing her attention again. Her green eyes meet my blue ones with sadness, the edges of her eyes brimming with tears. Finally, I see the real Bree. The whole Bree.

"Life is about taking risks. I know this is going to sound cliche and cringey but I'm going to say it. Not to torture you but to get it through your head how you shouldn't waste time. If you really love him, if you care for him, you will fight for him. It doesn't matter what other people think because all that matters is the two of you. You need to live right now to the max otherwise you will regret it for the rest of your life." I pause for a second to think about my next words.

"I get you are feeling hurt - trust me, I've been there for two years and it sucks - but you need to overcome that hurt for the guy you love. If you can see yourself with him in the future, if you see yourself happy, you need to tell him everything. Don't give up, fight for your happiness. Fight for the person you love. It's going to be scary, there is always going to be that possibility of no but when sometimes, you need to take that risk for the long term. Don't let fear take away your happiness and love. " When I finish, I exhale with relief. I finally got that off of my chest.

I realized that that speech wasn't just for Bree but for me as well. I do need to overcome everything, including fear. I'm letting doubt about so much cloud everything with Max. I know I'm not ready to date him yet but that doesn't mean I can't be stuck like this forever. I can slowly move forwards towards love.

But first, I need to get to know this new Max better. He's changed, just like I have. And we need to learn everything about each other again before I completely give him my heart.

I'm knocked out of my thoughts when Bree tackles me with a heartwarming hug. Her thin pale arms wrap tightly around my waist and she snuggles her head in my shoulder. Instantly, I respond to her hug, equally affectionate.

"Thank you," she whispers in a low voice.

"Anytime," I reply.

Bree pulls away and wipes her eyes. She composes herself and smiles happily.

"I'm going to go and get my man now." She states and without another word, she's marching off to Harry who is waiting in the car.

I smile, watching her walk off.

"So when are you going to get your man?" A male's voice asks from behind me. I jump and swivel around to see Max. He stands in all of his handsome glory with his trademark smirk.

I give him a glare for scaring me. "When I feel I'm ready for him."

"Well, I hope its soon because I'm not very patient."

I roll my eyes, trying to prevent the smile that wants to come on my face. Stupid Max with his remarks.

"Now is her majesty ready for her carriage?" He asks in a fake British accent. To add to the effect, he bows.

I confidently stroll past Max, slapping his head for his silliness. He yelps in pain but quickly recovers.

"That wasn't very nice," he remarks once he's caught up with me. I don't respond, only continuing to walk through the car park to the rest of the group so I can wish them goodbye. "By the way, your face was so cute when you were watching the film. I had to refrain myself from pinching those adorable cheeks."

And that's when I attack him.

What is it with girls lunging or tackling boys today?

20

20 | Jealousy, Space Bowls, and Some Sunshine

When the weekend finally came, I was more than happy. Just five days at school was enough to physically and mentally drain me. Also, seeing Max after two years definitely contributed to my exhaustion. I feel mentally drained from his presence - and his cockiness.

My parents both noticed my state and decided to leave me alone for the weekend. Its now Saturday and I spent the whole of the morning sleeping in my comfy bed. I don't need any man, not when I have my bed who will always be here for me.

My mom informed me that they are both going out later today so I'm pondering whether I should invite the gang round or not. The dilemma is that Max will hear about the party because I know Molly is dead set on getting us back together and will come. I don't know if I want him coming to my home. We agreed we are friends but I don't think we are at the 'you can come and hang out at my house' bit yet.

I could always spend time with myself and binge watch something on Netflix. There's a TV show called Money Heist that sounds quite interesting.

Before I can come to a decision, my phone rings. Eagerly, I pick it up and answer, not bothering to check who it is.

"This is Ava speaking, how can I help you?" I answer, my voice sounding a lot higher than I expected.

"Well hello Ava, I know you're going to hate me saying this but the sound of your cheery voice has already made my day a lot better." A deep voice that I recognize greets me on the other side of the line.

Instantly, I straighten my posture at the sound of Max's voice. How did he get my number? Unless someone gave it to him...somebody who has made it her mission to have me back with Max. Molly.

That little minx.

"Max," I sigh, tiredly. "I must say, I shouldn't be surprised that Molly gave you my number. It appears my friends are already plotting against me."

Max snorts on the other side of the line at my statement. His perception of this current situation is very different from mine. Whilst he thinks me having his number is a blessing, I see it as a curse.

"Me? plotting?" Max questions, in a voice of disbelief. "Never. I love you too much to do such things."

Whilst my heart hammers in my chest at his flirting, my brain thinks something very different. He claims he couldn't do something horrendous yet he did - he broke my freaking heart. A big part of me wants to snap at him for saying that but I refrain myself from doing so. We are making some progress towards peace, if I went and blurted out my thoughts, we would move ten steps back.

Oddly, that's something I don't want to happen.

"Whatever you say, Max. So do you want to tell me why you called? Come to harass me again?" I inquire. I'm actually interested as to why he's called me. If it's for a chat, I guess it wouldn't do any harm.

"Well Sunshine," Max clears his throat dramatically. Once again, my heart constricts in my chest at my old nickname. The one he gave me on holiday two years ago. The one I pretended to despise but really loved. "I'm here to ask if you are free later. We can meet up, just the two of us... or we could meet up with your new group of friends?"

And now I'm back to the dilemma.

Do I want to hang out with him alone or with the rest of the gang?

"Oh - uh." I splutter. I honestly don't know what I want. If this were a movie right now, I would have the cliche mini-me dressed as a devil on one of my shoulders, whilst a mini-me dressed as an angel on the other shoulder. They would both be weighing the advantages and disadvantages to me accepting to meet with him alone.

I can almost imagine what would happen. The devil me would say life is all about taking risks, about being confident and not thinking about anything else. The devil would be on team going out with Max alone.

However, the angel side of me would say that its too soon, Max could make a move on me.

But then there's a small part of me that is screaming I am just reading too much into everything. It's not like I'm debating whether to marry Max or not. It's only meeting up for a while, to do normal teenage stuff.

"Ava? You still there?" I hear Max's voice in my ear, bringing me back to reality.

Max knows what I want and despite his mistakes, he wouldn't do something I'm not comfortable with. He knows if he messes up, I will never speak to him again. I don't think he's willing to make a stupid mistake.

I trust Max. I know I do.

"Alright, I'll go out with you." I eventually answer his first question. "What do you have in mind?"

"Oh Sunshine, that's for me to know and you to find out," Max replies, his voice laced with cockiness. Even though I can't see him, I can imagine him grinning ear to ear right now. "I'll be at your house in one hour."

"But you don't know where I li -" Max cuts me off by hanging up on the phone. I purse my lips at his rudeness and roll my eyes. I predict that in forty-five minutes, I'm going to get a text message asking where I live.

***

"You look gorgeous." Max compliments as soon as I open my front door.

I flash him a grateful smile, ignoring my stuttering heart. "Thanks. I'm surprised you managed to find my house."

Max smirks at my confusion and curiosity. "I had help."

"Oh," my eyebrows raise up. "And who decided to help you?"

I think I can already tell who helped him. "My magical, very helpful fairy godmother who goes by the name of Molly."

I chuckle at his response. That's definitely one way of describing the brunette who is helping more than I assumed.

"You ready?" He asks me and I nod my head, taking the keys off of the wall and my clutch. Shutting and locking the door, I make my way down the path to Max's black BMW. Like the gentleman he is, Max kindly opens his door, offering a hand to help me in. Gladly, I accept his help and get into my seat.

Max runs around the front of the car to the driver's seat and gets in. He buckles up and starts the ignition. The car roars to life, the engine sounding beautiful. I hum in delight and lean back in the leather seat. God knows how he can afford this car.

My eyes wander around the car, taking in its interior. I'm not going to lie, I'm jealous of Max right now. I dream of having a car like this.

"So where are we heading?" I question Max.

Max glances at my face, his brown eyes sparkling with mischief. "I'm not going to relent Ava. You'll just have to wait and see."

I huff and cross my arms stubbornly. Max grins in triumphant and accelerates out of his parking space. Whilst I aimlessly stare out of the window, marveling in the scenery.

***

Thirty minutes later, Max pulls into a free parking space. Anxiously I sit up in my seat, gazing out of the window to try and understand where I am. I gasp as I see the sign for a water park. Out of all the places Max could have taken me to, he takes me to a water park without ordering me to bring a swimming costume. Thanks, Max.

"Really?" I mutter with a sigh and get out of the car. The soft breeze blows a few strands of my hair over my face. Before I can brush them away, a tanned finger does it for me instead. My blue eyes flicker up to Max's brown eyes. He maintains eye contact with me as he tucks the strand of hair behind my ear slowly. Briefly, his hand makes contact with my ear, causing an assault of electricity to hit me.

Wordlessly, Max places his hand in mine and leads me to the building. I don't comment or give Max a snarky remark about holding my hand because friends do this too, right? They hold hands all of the time - like Rosie and I used to do it all of the time.

A twinge of guilt hits me at the thought of my best friend. I feel like I'm betraying her for doing this - spending time with Max. She would be biting my ear off is she heard about this. But since we're not even on speaking terms right now, I don't think I'm going to get a scolding anytime soon.

Max opens the doors and I step in. My nose is overcome with the strong smell of chlorine and my ears hear the screams of girls. There's a short cue that we have to line up for.

"Max, I don't have my swimming costume, I can't go swimming," I tell him, eyeing the bags everyone else has.

I hear Max sigh and let go of my hand. I open my mouth to ask him where he's going but when I see the rack of swimming costumes he's walking over to, my mind connects the dots. Does he even know my size though? I swear if he gets a costume that's too big for me, I will be furious.

Max snatches a one suit costume for me and a pair of trunks for himself, along with two towels and some shampoo. By the time he makes it back, we are next in line to pay.

"Two adult bands please," he asks the woman politely. She smiles flirtatiously at Max and types something on the keyboard with her long, manicured nails.

I must admit, Max is undeniably handsome. There is no doubt in my mind that he receives look from women like the receptionist all of the time. I know that women want to be with him. Hell, I hear the girls in my new school talking about how hot he is in the corridors.

My blood boils at the thought of Max being with another girl. I only feel one thing at the very thought of it. Jealously.

And I hate it.

"Here you are," the young woman hands us the bands. Her hand lingers on Max's hands, whilst her grey eyes flicker up to his. I suddenly have the urge to rip her fingers off of his skin and slap her cheek. But it appears Max doesn't like what she's doing either because he yanks his hand away and glares harshly at the woman.

She visibly gulps and sits back at her seat, turning her attention away from him. Max smirks victoriously and grabs my hand again, dragging me to the changing rooms.

Without a word, Max gives me my costume and ushers me into the free cubicle. I get changed into the outfit and look at the costume. I'm shocked that Max not only got the right size but he got a costume that doesn't show off too much. My cleverage isn't hanging out, its snuggly in the costume. The costume fits my body like a second skin, showing off my curves.

I bite my lip in wonder at the thought of Max possibly liking my outfit. Would he be pleased with how I look or does he prefer girls with more boobs and butt? Just because he loves me, doesn't mean he likes my body...

Its stupid how I think like this but every single person has her insecurities. Deep down, I know Max loves me and how I look yet I still fear he doesn't.

With a deep breath, I come out of the changing room and dump my clothing in a locker. I'm glad I shaved and showered last night. Having hairy legs would be awkward.

Max soon joins me and dumps his stuff in the same locker and locks it. I attach the bracelet with the key around my wrist and follow Max out of the changing rooms to the water park. I gasp in excitement when I see the thrilling waterslides I'm going to go on.

"This place looks amazing!" I squeal and happily clap my hands. I probably resemble a little kid right now but I don't care.

Max chuckles at my behavior and places a hand on my waist. I take no notice of it, too absorbed by the waterpark.

"What do you want to go on first?" Max whispers in my ear in a low tone. My eyes dart from each water slide. I have no clue what I want to go on first.

"Uh...how about that one?" I point to a slide called The Space Bowl. The slide is like a space bowl where you slide down it and then spin in a large bowl before dropping into a deep water tank. It looks really exciting.

"Let's go then." He says and I walk over to the steps that lead to the line.

Deciding to go out with Max was the best decision I made so far since I came to this town.

21

21 | Surprise?

Since the trip to the water park two weeks ago, Max and I have grown a lot closer. Our time at the park was spent laughing and joking, acting like we were close buddies. There wasn't any awkwardness between us - which I was very surprised about.

The gang has noticed how close we've gotten. I spend a lot of time with Max, in lessons and out. We often go to Mama Coco's to talk or do homework.

Speaking of the gang, I've also grown closer with a lot of them. The boys are now aware of what happened between Max and I. When they first found out, Lawrence, Harry, Luke, and Josh started getting really protective of me when I'm around Max. It warmed my heart to see them care about me so much.

Max had to have a long talk with them about his intentions and how much he regretted what he did. Apparently, according to Josh, he was on the verge of tears. The boys ended up warning Max to not pull a stunt like that again. Max promised on his mothers' heart that he wouldn't; so things went back to normal.

Molly and Bree have also managed to worm their way into my heart. I've shared some things I never thought I would share before. Them, along with Max, bring back the old Ava. Well, parts of her.

For example, I'm nicer to strangers. Before, I would give them an expressionless face because I didn't see the point in being nicer to someone who wouldn't return it. But now, I see past that. I'm happier; I want to spread that to everyone else.

"Yo Ava," Harry calls, walking into our Psychology class. I recently found out that he was in this class with me but he had bunked the last couple of lessons. To say I was shocked that Harry, the shy nerd bunked is an understatement. My guess is that he tries to avoid this class because of a certain red-head in it. Bree.

"Wassup Harry?" I greet, dragging the word 'wassup'. Harry and I recently had an interesting conversation about the film Scream and well, we now make jokes about it.

Harry shakes his head at my attempt and sits down next to me. His eyes stay focused solely on me and not on the redhead sat in front of me who refuses to turn around with him there.

Bree admitted that after her spontaneous plan to tell Harry she's sorry, she backed out. She claims her nerves got the better of her but I think its more than that. So she has resorted back to pretending he doesn't exist.

"Please don't do that again," Harry says, almost looking tortured at my attempt.

I pout and place my hand on my chest where my heart is. "You wound me, Harry. You honestly do."

"Whatever A - "Harry's cut off by pompous, asshole psychology teacher who has the worst attitude ever.

"Quiet down you brats." He yells, capturing everyone's attention. Quickly, everyone sits in their seats and shuts their gobs, giving him frightened faces. Once, Gerald Finn, a goody two shoes pointed out that Mr. Limp - our psychology teacher - couldn't call us brats and he ended up in detention for three weeks. He's still going to it; absolutely hates it. "Now I want you to read about the working memory model in memory. When you've read through it, you can produce a pretty poster of it."

And with that, Mr. Limp collapses onto his comfy chair and starts to scroll through his phone. I roll my eyes at his behavior and begin to read through the interesting working memory model.

Halfway through reading it, a finger pokes my shoulder. Annoyed, I turn to face Harry with an unimpressed expression.

"Yes?" I whisper, eyeing Mr. Limp through the corner of my eye. He hates people talking when we are doing work, claiming silence is the best for everyone - everyone being him.

"Is the working memory model short-term memory or long-term memory?" Harry asks me.

I sigh and run a hand through my hair. "It's short-term memory." Harry nods his head, thanking me and then continues to read it. I try to do the same but I can't seem to focus back on it. My thoughts drift to Max and what he was like this morning. He seemed livelier, happier than usual.

I make a note to ask him later.

"Psst, Ava," I hear Bree's voice call quietly. I snap my eyes up in front of me and raise an eyebrow.

"You called," I mumble.

"At the end of the day, can you come to the gym changing rooms?" She asks me, looking excited about something.

I frown and answer her question with a question. "Why?"

Bree rolls her eyes and leans further back in her chair but not before checking what Mr. Limp is doing. "Because there's a surprise for you. Just go, don't question it."

I sigh and nod my head in agreement. She said its a surprise so it should be exciting. Perhaps this has something to do with Max and why he was giddy today.

When the bell rings, I'm more than happy to leave. I'm not going to lie, I'm really excited about later today. I wonder what Max has in store for me - at least, I think its Max that has done this.

I practically skip to my next class, smiling. A few people I have become acquainted with send me cheerful smiles and wave. I happily return them.

My whole attitude reminds me of the old Ava, who would say hello to every single person. Perhaps Max's promise to show me how 'amazing' I am has also brought out the best in me.

When I arrive at English literature, Max gestures for me to come and sit next to him. As if I would sit somewhere else. I enjoy his presence, I look forward to seeing him.

"Sunshine, how lovely to see you," Max smirks and swivels on his seat to properly face me.

"Isn't it always nice to see me?" I ask him, arching an eyebrow.

"Oh, of course." He replies confidently. His chocolate eyes eye me up and down, assessing my outfit. "You 're just particularly lovely today."

I roll my eyes at his attempt at being charming. We both know that I look the same as usual. I'm wearing what I usually wear - a crop top and a pair of black skinny jeans. Which is my usual attire.

Could this have something to do with the surprise later?

It could well be. That's the only reason I can think of that has Max acting like this. Gosh, my curiosity is eating me alive. What on earth could it be? I try to process all of my options. Since it's on the soccer field, most options are limited.

If it turns out to be some cliche moment where he asks me to be his girlfriend or to ask me out on a date, I will smack him on the head so hard.

But you're assuming the surprise has something to do with Max. My conscience says, reminding me that it may not. Bree was the one who asked me to go there, not Max. For all I know, he has nothing to do with it. He could be in the dark like me.

"So, did you ever finish the Macbeth homework?" I ask him, pulling out my Macbeth copy and my two-page essay on fate. It certainly wasn't fun writing that yesterday after putting it off the last couple of days.

Max snorts, "do you really think I would do that?"

I shrug my shoulders. "I mean, you are the unannounced bad boy but that doesn't mean you don't do your homework."

Max gives me an offended look, almost wounded.

"Bingo!" Max hurray's, throwing his hands up in the air. "Have you even met my parents?" He exclaims and I arch an eyebrow at his question. Does he not recall the meals that we had with his parents during that summer? "Oh wait, stupid question - never mind."

I shake my head, laughing.

"Anyways, the answer to your question," Max leans closer to me, after quickly glancing around the room suspiciously. As if we were exchanging nuclear launch codes. "I did. But shush, you can't tell anybody that."

I roll my eyes and lean back, my eyes scanning over my work. I could almost be proud of my work - after spending many hours cussing about it. I have never completely enjoyed Shakespeare but Macbeth is a really interesting play. Despite the fact, I don't really understand half of it.

When our teacher steps into the classroom, the room quietens down and I relax in my seat. Max sends me a smirk and then proceeds to get his work out for the teacher.

"Right can everybody put their homework on their desks for me to collect. Whilst I'm collecting them, I would like someone to explain, using quotes from the play, how Lady Macbeth is portrayed in Macbeth." Our teacher asks, waiting for a response. Every single student lowers their head and pretends to be busy with something else, including me. I doodle on my empty notepad, lightly shading in a circle.

"Well then." He clears his throat. "I'll just have to pick someone. How about...Ava."

Dammit!

Never have I wanted to cuss at a teacher so much before. I despise sharing my work, partly because I go red just at uttering one word.

Taking a shaky breath, I try to rack my brain for some sort of plausible answer. "Right so, when we are first introduced to Lady Macbeth, she speaks about death. 'Come you spirits' suggests her summoning dark figures, which can relate to the witches who used spirits to find the prophecy. In her monologue at the beginning, she also speaks about becoming a man, 'unsex me here', implying she wants to be more powerful since society was very patriarchal back then. She also speaks about 'passag[ing] to remorse' to stop pain and compassion. To stop feeling. This can portray her as evil because if she does kill or has a hand in the killing, she won't feel guilty about it. Thus, showing what is considered an evil trait. Finally, at the end of her monologue, she says 'nor heaven peep through the blanket of the dark' suggesting she doesn't want innocent, good spirits to see her evil. Perhaps she thinks she can still go to heaven despite doing evil acts. Therefore, she can be seen as a manipulator and well..evil."

Once I'm finished, I release a sigh of relief and slouch back in my chair. I can feel my cheeks reddening at the sight of some people staring at me.

My teacher grunts in approval and starts writing something on the board.

"Nice going smart-ey pants." I hear Max congratulate beside me. Flipping him off for the nickname, I grip my pen and begin writing what's on the board.

22

22 | How I Really Feel

"O'gentle lady, 'tis not for you to hear what I can speak. The repet— " I angrily cut Max off by smacking the back of his head. In surprise and shock, Max flinches and mutters an 'ouch.' "What was that for? I was only reciting some Shakespeare quotes."

I arch an eyebrow and give him an innocent smile. "Oh were you? My bad."

Max presses his lips together and narrows his eyes. I mentally dust off my shoulder at my slick reply and focus back on the busy hallways. Without another word, Max walks beside me with a scowl etched on his face.

"Aww, did I upset the poor Max?" I coo patronizingly.

Max doesn't reply, he only huffs. I snigger at his behavior. Apparently, acting like a five-year-old is Max's specialty.

"Ava, can I ask you something?" Max seriously asks. I'm taken aback by his sudden change in attitude yet curious to know what brought it on.

I smile, reassuringly. "Sure."

Max rolls his shoulders, an action he does when he is nervous about something or doesn't know how to put it into words. Its surprising how much I can remember about him, how I what he does in certain situations.

"Do you think you will ever be able to be back with me? Do you see a future for the both of us?"

I stop mid-stride in the packed hallways. Max, who is a few steps ahead of me, stops as well and turns around to face me. Some people walking in the hall-ways scowl at me for getting in the way but I ignore them.

My mind is too submerged in thoughts about what Max just said. Once upon a time, I saw a bright future with Max and I. Two years ago, if someone asked me where I would be in twenty years time, I would respond with something like 'married to Max, with beautiful children and a stable job'. But now...I have no idea at all.

When I was seven, I had everything thought out. In my head, I saw myself as a vet. I imagined living in a nice house, with a garden full of flowers and children's toys. When I was seven, my dream was to live happily ever after.

But I was naive. So naive.

At the age of sixteen, I pictured what my house would look like - with Max. I had a clear image of the house and I dreamed about my wedding.

But at the age of eighteen, I have no freaking clue. I was hurt - hurt badly. The prospect of marriage and children seems daunting. I don't think I want to go throw any sort of heartbreak again.

Sadly, I can see myself living in a cozy one bedroom apartment alone. Whilst I like having time alone, I also like spending my time with people. I'm a people person. I value spending my time with friends.

They hold me together, they keep me sane. Grounded. I need them more than they need me. When Rosie didn't reply to any of my messages, I was hurt. I still am. I don't know if my best friend is going to talk to me ever again; I hate it. A part of me is pissed that she's ignoring me on purpose because I did something she didn't approve of. Another part of me is understanding.

Maybe I should try calling her aga -

"Yo, Ava?" Max interferes with my thoughts, waving his calloused hand in front of my face. Flinching in shock, I give Max a sheepish smile when I recover.

"Sorry," I apologize, feeling my cheeks heat up. "I just got lost in my thoughts." I explain and bitterly add quietly: "again."

Max presses his lips together, "that's okay. So whats your answer?"

I blink. "Answer?"

"For the question, I asked you," Max replies, rolling his eyes, annoyed. Or at least, I thought he was annoyed by my lack of attention until his lips began curving upwards.

"Oh," I say, dumbly. "Right, yes. I—um—I." I stutter pathetically like a blubbering piece of fish. How is it I always end up like this in front of Max? How does he still have this effect on me? Clearing my throat, I try to answer again. "I—I don't know Max. Honestly, I'm not even sure what my future looks like. Let alone a future with other people in my life. I'm confused. I used to have all of this planned out but after...well, you know, I became somebody who lives in the fast lane instead. I go with the flow."

Max lowers his head, sadly. My heart aches at the thought of him being sad.

"Listen," I start, touching his chin and gently lifting it up. His brown orbs stare into mine, searching for something. "Just because I don't have a plan anymore doesn't mean you won't be in it. Maybe you will be in my life, maybe I will date you. Who knows. I certainly don't. But don't be disheartened. You may find someone else, another girl who makes you happy."

As much as it pains me to say those words, I have to get through to him in some way. I'm beginning to get over him. I'm happy that he's in my life and I won't lie, he has made me brighter. But perhaps we weren't meant to be. Perhaps all we had was a connection and we were only stepping stones.

Max's face falls, whatever gleam in his eyes burning out. He swallows and clenches his jaw.

"Right." He spits and roughly drags a hand through his brown hair. I watch him, memorizing him.

"That summer was the best I had." I blurt out before I can think twice. His eyes snap to mine, confused but I ignore it and continue. "You showed me what love is, what heartbreak is. That's how I know what we had was true because of that pain afterward. I don't regret it though." He silently watches me, assessing me. My hand reaches up to touch his cheek; when he doesn't flinch back, I cup his cheek and step closer and bury my head in his neck. His whole body stills for a brief moment. "We were young and we made mistakes. But that's what everyone does - they make mistakes and then they learn from them. I know that now and I'm glad it did happen."

"Me too," Max says, huskily. "What I did was wrong and I know that now. And yes, I need to start accepting that we might not be together again. All I want is for you to be happy."

I smile and cling to his top. "I am. Right now, I have amazing friends, I talked to my ex-boyfriend and I know more about myself. All I have to do is talk to Rosie and help Bree out."

Max chuckles. "I think my mission is going ahead as planned."

"Really?"

"Oh, definitely."

***

"Where is the surprise you were on about?" I question Max once we make it to the empty field. My eyes search the area, trying to pick anything out that would relate to it. Unfortunately, I come up with nothing.

"Dammit, she bailed." Max curses under his breath, so quietly I barely get it.

"I don't see anything," I remark. "Is someone coming?"

Max shakes his head, upset. "Not anymore, let's just go."

He places his hand on the lower part of my back and guides me back into school. I glance over my shoulder one last time, trying to figure out who was supposed to come.

***

One week later.

"Guess what."

I flick my eyes up to Max who is lounging on one of the sofas in the library. "What?"

"My parents want to meet your parents for dinner this weekend." He answers.

"Oh my gosh, really?" I ask, feeling excited at the prospect of seeing his parents again. I missed them so much, they were like my second parents.

Max's parents are the definition of a polar opposite couple but they are perfect for each other. They always treated me like their daughter. Whenever Max said something rude to me or teased me, they would say the funniest things that would embarrass him. I would be laughing so hard for hours after hearing them tell a humiliating story about him that tears would be falling down my cheeks.

"Yep, my mom is arranging it with your mom."

I put the book I'm reading down and fist pump into the air. I'm already excited about next week.

"Hey Max, this Friday, do you want to go to a party with me and the gang?" I ask him, hoping he will say yes. Over the last few days, Max has basically become officially accepted into the group. We are all friends—minus Bree and Harry—and we already have plans for upcoming weekends. This weekend, we want to go to a party. Lawrence offered to be the person who stays sober to look after the group meaning the rest of us can get drunk.

"That sounds great. I haven't been to one in a while, it's about time I busted out some moves." He jokes, doing a dance move to prove his point about not doing one in a while. I giggle at his awful attempt and blow out a breath.

"Oh god, please don't tell me I have to witness that," I whine, already envisioning him dancing. Long story short, the dude has two left feet.

Max rolls his eyes and gets his phone out of his pocket. "Maybe you and I can dance together for a song?"

My eyes shift to him at his suggestion. "Hmm, as long as you don't step on my feet - sure."

Max smiles brightly whilst I read the first line of the next page. God, I hate history.

23

23 | Parties and Kisses

My back is pushed against the wall roughly but I don't care. His hands are placed on my hips tightly, keeping me against the wall. I grab onto his soft brown hair, tugging on it. He groans huskily into my mouth, his lips pushed against mine. Our kisses are sloppy yet passionate. We are both desperate for each other, to feel each other.

His hands move down to my thighs and effortlessly, he lifts me up. I wrap my legs around his torso, greedily and hungrily taking him in.

Max moves us from the wall and onto the bed, slowly lowering me. Eventually, we stop our kissing to breath. I suck in a handful of oxygen, letting my lungs breath again.

Max does the same, from above me. He stares at me with a fire in his brown eyes and that's when I realize what is happening.

Shocked, I scramble away from him and sit on the end of the bed. Confused, Max sits down too, hurt in his eyes. My brain registers everything that just happened, how I made the first move and kissed him with such...ferocity.

"Oh my god," I mumble under my breath, my head feeling a bit woozy. Exactly how much alcohol did I have? "Oh my god, oh my god," I repeat, rubbing my face tiredly.

"Ava," Max whispers, moving to sit right in front of me. Hesitantly, Max moves to hold my hand. When I don't flinch away or slap him, he clutches it. The sparks I usually feel give me comfort at this moment.

"Please, just...be quiet for a second. I need to gather my thoughts." I murmur, attempting to grasp what I did.

My mind replays everything that happened, starting with earlier on today.

"Okay." I hear Max say. And with that, my memories take over.

***

Five hours earlier

"I really like that dress," Bree says to me, eyeing the sea-blue dress I'm putting above my clothing. I hum in agreement, loving the color and design of it. The dress will definitely complement and bring out my eyes. I got that dress as a present a couple of years ago from my auntie who I never see. She thought I was bigger than I was so she bought it in a bigger size. So I couldn't wear it back then. But now I'm taller, I can wear it.

Molly searches my wardrobe for something to wear too. I invited both of the girls around my house so we could get ready for the party later. Bree said she might need help with her hair so I offered to do it for her. Molly also claimed she had no dresses that were 'party-like' so I said I would lend her one. Hence why we are at my house.

"Hey Ava, what about this?" Molly asks, holding up a black, sequin dress. I envision her wearing the dress and nod my head. It would show off those amazing curves she likes to keep hidden. I have a feeling she doesn't like showing off her body because Josh is overprotective of her.

"You will look stunning in that. You have such an amazing body, you should never hide it out of embarrassment." I tell her, truthfully.

I remember when I used to be like Molly. I was insecure about my body and looks so I tried to avoid going to parties. Then I met Rosie and she got me out of my shell and took me to parties.

After Max, instead of feeling defeated and worried about myself, I felt a bit better about myself. Sure, I don't think I'm the prettiest girl in the world but who does? Everybody feels unsure about their looks.

Now, I will go to parties and enjoy myself. I don't care if a boy is looking at me with lust or if the girls were giving me looks of disgust. They can go and look at me like that because they will never affect me the way they want to.

Huh, if Max were to hear this right now he would be like 'see! I told you my plan was working!' Maybe his silly speech is finally getting to me. I am stronger.

A couple of days ago, I stood up to cheerleaders. When I was with Max, I would rely on him to tell girls to bugger off when they approached him - asking for his number - because I was too afraid. But when I stood up to them, I did it because I knew they were being awful and I had the chance to stop them.

I even managed to forgive Max.

"Ugh, you guys all have super pretty dresses and I don't. I bet I will end up going in jeans and a t-shirt." Bree complains.

Laughing at her, I drag her to my wardrobe and help her find an outfit.

***

An hour later, we all pile out of Bree's car and stare at the building. Already, I can hear the loud thumping of music and I can see the red cups littered on the grass.

"Holy moly, this party looks amazing." Molly gushes, gawking at the party. I'm starting to get the impression that she doesn't go to parties very often.

"Molly, how often do you go to parties?" I ask her, watching her out of the corner of my eye.

Molly shrugs, "if I go to parties, Josh has to be around me. He doesn't trust guys."

I give her a sympathetic look, honestly feeling so sorry for her that her brother restricts her from having fun.

"Let's go then." Bree hollers with a glint in her eye. Nodding in agreement, we all walk into the house.

When I step in, I look around the place to get a feeling of it. The party is a typical one, there's a dance floor in the living room, a mini bar in the kitchen and a ping pong table set up in the games room. There are lights coming from the garden so I'm guessing something is going on there as well.

The whole house is packed with drunk teenagers, each looking for fun.

"Oh my god! Let's dance!" Molly says, an excited look plastered on her face. Laughing, I let her hold my hand and drag me to the dance floor. Molly also takes Bree's hand, pulling her too.

A new song starts, one that I recognize as Hung Up by Madonna. I remember the time when this song came on when I was at a party with Rosie. We danced like maniacs on the dance floor, kicking everybody else off. The both of us laughed like there was no tomorrow, getting wasted.

Swallowing the memory, I push that back and try to focus on enjoying tonight.

The three of us make a miniature circle and begin swaying our bodies to the beat, giggling. At one point, Lawrence heads over with drinks. We all down them quickly and continue dancing. The boys join in too, even Harry who is remaining sober tonight.

After several drinks and many weird dance moves, I can officially say I am drunk.

"Guys, I think that guy is looking at me." Molly slurs, trying to point at someone, or more like something. Her body staggers; Josh is quick to grab onto her. I laugh when I can just about make out the cute teddy bear on the table.

Josh, who is only tipsy, whispers something into Molly's ear that has her protesting in his arms. She tries to get out of his hold but he doesn't let her.

"I don't want to go. I want to go and flirt with the cute thing over there." She claims, referring to the teddy bear. I burst into a fit of giggles, leaning onto Lawrence who wraps an arm around my shoulder.

"She's totally drunk," I say in Lawrence's ear, laughing at what I said.

Lawrence chuckles at what I said and shakes his head.

"I think you are drunk too," Lawrence tells me.

Pulling away, I pout. "No, I'm not. I'm only a bit tipsy."

With that, I step away from Lawrence and lose myself in the crowds. They want to take me home now but I don't want to. I want to party more. To me, it still feels really early. If Rosie was here, she would be the one encouraging me to party more.

At some point during the night, I end up dancing with some guy. I don't recognize who he is but I'm pretty sure he is drunk. We sway to the music, his hands on my hips and mine on his shoulders.

His head lowers to mine and he captures my lips with his. His lips feel rough against mine as he fiercely mushes our lips together. The thing is, I don't feel sparks like I want to. My heart isn't going mad and my blood is rushing. I just feel...sad.

Before I can pull away from him, he's ripped off of me by someone. I shouldn't have been surprised when I saw Max standing there with a furious expression on his face. Yet, I was.

Max fists the guy's t-shirt around his hand and pulls him closer. I watch Max hiss something in his ear and the guy nods his head with a scared face. Satisfied, Max lets the man go and turns his attention to me.

When I see the hurt in his eyes, I feel guilty. He has been trying to prove to me how he made a mistake and I messed up by kissing another guy. The worst thing is, I wished I was kissing Max.

Max heads over to me and picks me up bridal style, walking out of the hot and sweaty room and upstairs.

He kicks open a door that is slightly ajar and places me gently on the bed. When I'm safely deposited on the bed, Max stands up tall and crosses his arms with an enraged look.

"What on earth were you doing Ava?" He asks, anger clear in his tone. Gulping, I wonder how I will get out of this.

24

24 | Parties and Kisses (part 2)

"What on earth were you doing Ava?" He asks, anger clear in his tone. Gulping, I wonder how I will get out of this.

My mouth opens and closes in shock. I don't know what was thinking. The answer is: I wasn't thinking. I just...kissed him. I didn't think about the repercussions, I didn't consider what it would do to Max. I just kissed him.

Max patiently waits for an answer, staring at me expectantly.

"I -" Pausing, I think of what to say. Swallowing, I attempt to say something to him. "Oh god, I messed up."

Max doesn't respond. In fact, he doesn't do anything other than stand in front of the bed, watching. His intense gaze never unwavering, always on me. I'm beginning if he's looking at me or looking at me.

"It's almost funny. You are the one who usually mucks up but this time I did. I got drunk and kissed some guy knowing you have feelings for me. God, that makes me such a bitch." I say, light-heartedly, trying to ease the obvious tension in the room.

Max doesn't laugh.

"Oh come on, I tried to make a joke," I sigh.

I stand up, feeling slightly woozy and stumble my way to Max. Just as I'm about to reach Max, I trip on a bit of bed cover that is hanging on the ground. Max is quick to catch me, wrapping his arms around my waist.

His face hovers over mine, so close to me. I move my head closer to him, executing the first move. But before I can kiss him, Max hoists me up and puts me back on the bed. Disappointment fills my face and

I do something I never thought I would do in front of Max. I guess you can blame the alcohol for that.

I cry.

I cry, with hot tears running down my cheeks and curl up into a fetal position. I cry because I'm not as strong as I like to admit.

Sobbing, I think about all of the mistakes I've made, the bad things I've done. What I've said.

I am so lost in my thoughts, that I don't notice Max coming over to me until he uncurls me and picks me up. Gently, he places me on his lap and softly runs a hand through my knotty hair. I start sobbing into his chest, leaving my wet tears on his top.

For several moments, Max lets me have this moment. For a short while, he lets me have my moment to break down.

"Ssh," Max whispers into my ear, rocking me back and forth like a baby. When I run out of tears, I begin to hiccup. Max mutters comforting and soothing words into my hair, kissing my temple. "It's going to be okay. You're going to be fine."

Oddly enough, I believe his words. Perhaps its because I'm drunk or maybe its because they are coming from Max.

"I'm an awful person. I'm so mean." I state, my heart plummeting when I realize how true it is.

Looking up, I see Max frowning to himself. "What do you mean? You are one of the nicest people I know."

I nearly snort at his words but refrain myself from doing so.

Shaking my head, I fiddle with my hands. "I'm not. I was a complete bitch to you when I saw you. I called you words I didn't mean. I pushed you away. Its a miracle you're here right now, consoling me. You should be downstairs having fun with a girl who deserves you."

"No, no, no. Don't you dare say those things, Ava." Max practically insists. "You were hurt, I understand that. Hell, I would probably act like that too if I was in your position. Its a miracle you forgave me. And I'm glad you pushed me away. It only made me want to persist you more. Ava, you are so strong. You are amazing, beautiful and smart. You are so kind too, you help others out. I know you are trying to help Bree and Harry out - yes, I see something happened between them.

"Sunshine, I don't deserve you. You are above my league. The very fact you could be friends with me shows how you can put everything past us and give me a second chance. You put on a brave face and did something remarkable. God, you are so blind." He groans softly, resting his chin on my hair.

Electricity crackles around us, on my skin. My heart thumps and pumps so fast, with exhilaration and love.

I want to cry again. But not with sadness, disappointment. But with relief and love. God, so much love.

Sniffling, I rub my nose and wipe the single, happy tear, that streaks down my flushed face.

Max's attention resumes back to my face. He sends me a confused look, worried.

Laughing slightly, I answer him to relieve him of worrying anymore. "It's a happy tear. You...god, you have such a way with words. It's not even fair. You make me feel so special and one in a kind. God, now I do feel awful. But thanks, I really needed that. Sometimes our insecurities, doubts, and worries can catch up with us. I think the alcohol played a big part in it too."

Max nods his head in understanding and rubs circles on my arm.

"Max?" I ask, in a croaky voice. My throat still feels hoarse from all of my wailing.

Max hmms softly and I continue. "Can you kiss me?"

When Max doesn't respond, I twist in his lap and cup his cheeks, capturing his face. And then I smash my lips to his.

***

"I want you to know I loved you so much once. And whilst I'm not in the right place at the moment, one day I will be able to answer the question you are begging to hear." I say, breaking the silence that settled between us.

After thinking about what happened, from getting wasted to having a breakdown, I know what I have to say.

"I mess up sometimes. We all do, we are human. You messed up - two years ago." I begin, seeing Max flinch slightly in the corner of my eye. "I messed up by kissing that boy. We do it over and over. I think..."

I don't even know where I'm going with this. I don't know what I'm thinking.

Clearing his throat, Max says: "so we kissed. I think we should discuss that."

Sighing, I lie down on the bed. Max copies my movement, lying right next to me. Our hands are by our sides, inches apart.

"Yeah...maybe," I say, staring up at the ceiling.

"So..." Max awkwardly trails off.

I sigh. "I was drunk. I want to be honest with you Max. I'm not ready for a relationship, not yet. I want to experience life, single, independent. But I'm scared I will lose you."

"You won't," Max reassures but I don't believe him. He can't guarantee that.

"Max, what I am about to ask you is unfair and... wrong," I tell him, turning my face to stare at him. His brown eyes meet mine, a hidden uncertainty in them.

I'm starting to worry him.

With a deep breath, I begin. "I want - no, if you still want to go on a date with me, then ask me on our graduation day."

Finally uttering those words makes me realize how selfish they are. To ask anyone to do that, to save and wait is wrong and awful. I feel horrible and so self-centered.

But I have to make it clear to him that I'm not ready. I want - need - to focus on school. Since I have moved here, I've been searching for some colleges. I have a vague idea of the grades I need and I know that I need to put every part of me into studying. Being in a relationship will distract me.

Max doesn't deserve me to neglect him. He shouldn't have to listen to me yell at him, blame him for me failing classes.

We both need to focus on our future. We need to think about what we want. Max and I can want very different things, our paths may stop crossing and instead, they might start separating.

We both need to accept that.

Max sucks in a breath, shifting his position so he is staring back at the ceiling.

"Max, we are at the stage in our lives where we decide what we want," I explain. "We both need to make school our priority. We need to decide what we want to do - where we want to go. Being together right now will complicate everything. So that's why, when I have applied for colleges, graduated from high school, I want to go on a date with you. I know its selfish of me, cruel. You don't have to sign up for it, you don't have to wait. I will understand if you give up and let go. I will respect that."

Max listens intensively, taking in all of my words.

"But if we go to different universities, then what will we do?" Max questions, raising a point I was about to get to.

"Then we will come to that then. We can decide whether its a sign our paths no longer cross or we fight." I answer.

Max purses his lips together. "But what if I want to fight now."

"You don't." I immediately reply. He turns to me, arching an eyebrow. "You don't because you respect my choice. I do know you, Max. I know you will nod your head and accept my decision. Whether you ask me on that date next year, I don't know. And don't tell me now, I will wait. Leave it a mystery."

Finally feeling satisfied and content, I let my body relax. Everything that has been weighing on my shoulders has gone. Max now knows why I have been hesitant, doubtful.

"Thanks for being honest," Max says. "Are we going to remain friends then?"

I ponder on his question for a few seconds. I don't see why I can't. It would be unfair and unreasonable to dismiss him but continue to be friends with the others.

"Of course," I whisper.

"Well then, as your friend, I want to invite you on a trip tomorrow. Just you and me." Max declares.

"What? Why?" I inquire.

"You've said everything you needed to, now it's my turn. I'll be at your house tomorrow, at 7. Be ready." He informs me and gets up. "Oh and pack your swimming costume with a towel."

Word count: 1876

Please don't hate me or Ava. She has her reasons for acting like this!

I'm hoping to update another chapter in the next few days so look out for it. I want to have this book finished soon because I'm starting my second year of college next week (ugh). So not ready.

Also, I'm going to be posting the first chapter of Loving Hallie. I would really appreciate it if you checked it out. Thanks!

See you soon!!

25

25 | Honesty Isn't Always The Best Policy

When my alarm went off for the ridiculously early time of six am, I was not happy. Grumbling and groaning, I very reluctantly got out of my bed. My head was throbbing from last night, my muscles achy.

Faintly, I recall moments of the events that took place last night. Getting drunk was definitely something I can remember, along with kissing some guy and Max getting angry. What I can vividly remember is my conversation with Max.

Guilt overwashes me. I asked him to do something so selfless, to basically put his life on hold for me. I'm such a selfish person.

Tumbling out of my bed, I stumble over to my wardrobe and pick an outfit to wear. The first thing I pack when I'm putting my stuff in a bag is my swimming costume and a towel. Max specifically told me to bring that - though, I'm still completely unsure why.

My parents are still fast asleep in their room. Tonight we are going out for dinner with Max's family for a reunion meal. Wherever Max is taking me shouldn't be so far since we need to be back for eight.

Before I leave my room, I take an aspirin for the mild headache going on in my head. Scribbling a note on the fridge for my parents, I pour myself a cup of orange juice and pick an apple out from the fruit bowl. Not long after biting into my apple, a honk sounds. Smiling to myself, I down the orange juice and swing my bag over my shoulder.

Max is seated in his expensive, flashy car, waiting for me. I open the door and let the smell of new car fill my senses.

"Hi," I say, flashing him an uncertain smile. The feeling of apprehension stays with me. What if things begin to become awkward between us since the talk?

What if Max doesn't even want to be friends with me?

God, honesty isn't always the best policy.

Max turns to me, his handsome face expressionless. My shoulder slump in dread, my heart stopping momentarily.

"Are you okay?" He finally speaks, his eyes lightening up for a split moment.

Nodding my head, I pull the seatbelt over my body. "I have a bit of a headache but I took an aspirin so I should be fine. What-what about you?"

Max starts the engine, letting the sweet sound of the powerful engine resound through the empty area. I hope nobody heard it.

"Sure."

I turn to face him, chewing anxiously on my lip. What I really want to ask him is if he's still okay with what I said last night. Now that he's slept on it, he's had a lot of time to think about it. If he's not okay with my decision, he will probably tell me today.

Max switches on the radio to tune out the silence, keeping the current track on. When I hear the song Changes by Bowie, I sit up straighter and hum to the song. The song reminds me of my childhood when I used to love watching the film Shrek 2. Max notices my excited mood and chuckles.

And just like that, it's as if whatever tension in the car just disappears. Max joins in singing and together, with the windows down, we sway and sing.

I don't question when we get onto the highway or when we start getting further and further away from LA. Neither do I question when we turn off the highway and onto a long road.

We drive and drive, listening to the songs and bobbing our heads up and down. After a while of Max driving on a busy road, I look at the clock on the dashboard. I nearly gasp when I see that its nearly ten in the morning. We had been driving for three hours and I had no idea!

"Okay, I think its about time I ask this," I say. "Where are you taking me?"

"You'll see," he answers, his brown eyes glistening in mischief. I groan in annoyance and rest my head on the headrest. "We're close though."

Well, thank god for that.

Ten minutes later, Max pulls up into a car parking space. I spring up in my seat and take a good look at my surroundings. Its a gloriously sunny, cloudless day. There are a few birds, including seagulls, chirping. People in beach clothing, carrying tents and bags full of things pass us, laughing and smiling together.

The strong smell of the sea gives me the final bit of information I need to know we are close to the beach. In front of us, is a grassy, hill with remnants of sand. I'm guessing that beyond the small hill is the beach.

"We're at the beach?" I question, raising an eyebrow.

Max nods, unbuckling his seat belt. "I thought we should come back to a similar setting where we met."

My heart hammers in my heart, banging painfully against my chest. A part of my questions whether I made the right choice, especially when says simple things like this.

"Come on, we're wasting time," Max says and gets out of the car. Slowly, I follow his actions and get out. A small breeze brushes a few strands of my hair over my face. Pulling them away, I watch Max go to the boot of the car and get out a frisbee and a picnic basket. He comes over to me and holds his hand out for me, waiting for me to take it.

Without a second thought, I place my small hand in his larger one, savoring the pleasurable sparks I feel. Together, we walk to the small hill.

The sounds of waves crashing onto the shore can be heard before I even see the beach. Other people pass us, skipping happily to the beach. For late to September, the weather is still relatively good.

When we reach the top of the hill, I come to a halt so I can stare at the sight before me. The sun beats down onto the sand, giving it a certain shine. The bright, blue sea stuns me to the core. I have been to loads of beaches but this one, it has something to it. I don't know why but it captures my heart.

I wonder what it looks like in the evening when the sun sets.

"Beautiful isn't it?" Max asks me, whispering into my ear. Speechless, I nod my head. Words can't even describe this picturesque view.

Max tugs on my hand and pulls me onto the beach. Unconsciously, my toes curl into the warm sand. Together, we find a space closed off from everyone else. An isolated place where the two of us can be undisturbed.

I help Max unfold the towels and neatly place them on the sand. Its silent between, the crashing of the waves; the hungry sea gulls the only noise that can be heard.

"What's this beach called?"

Max turns to face me, "Manhattan Beach"

My mouth opens in an 'o' shape. Slowly, I lower my body onto the towel and stare at the blue sky. Max, who placed his towel right next to me, lies down as well. In silence, we think about what has been - who we are.

"I will always love you, know that Ava." Max blurts out quietly. Breathing in, I tilt my head to face him, putting a hand up to block the blaring sun.

"As will I," I respond. " But this is the right thing to do. It will prove to us whether we can live our lives as friends or if we are meant for each other."

"You know," Max starts, in a low voice. "When I first saw you, it wasn't in the hotel."

My head snaps to face him, shock evident on my face. I can recall the first time we met - the first time I saw him - and it was in the hotel. But apparently, that's not the case. Well, not for him.

"What -" I stop, swallowing. "Well, when did you first see me?"

"On that beach, the one similar to this." He gestures to the long beach that does resemble the one close to the hotel. "You were with your parents, laughing about something. When I saw you, my whole world stopped. Your laugh sounded so harmonious and angelic like it was too pure for this world. It's cheesy but so true."

My heart lips in my chest. "I like cheesy stuff."

Max meets my eyes, smirking. "I know."

"And - and you approached me after?" I question, with a hint of nervousness in my voice.

Max nods his head, his eyebrows puckering together as if he was deep in thought. "Yes. I followed you back to the hotel and waited for the perfect opportunity for me to meet you."

My body untenses and I relax, letting his words process. Who knew Max was a sweetheart from the beginning?

"If this arrangement is too awkward for you, we can always...resort to ignoring each other. Let each other move on with their lives." I suggest, portraying myself as calm externally.

Max stiffens for a brief moment. "Is that what you think is best?"

I turn my head back to look at the sky. Is it really what I want? Of course not. But what I want will prove to be a challenge. What if Max was to move on with someone else? How would I react?

I would hate it. I would feel jealous.

But I wouldn't act on it because I had my chance. If Max still wants to be with me, he knows when I'll be ready.

"I think that's for you to decide," I mutter, drawing circles on my flat stomach.

Max takes in a sharp breath. He quickly gets up, dusting off some sand on him.

"Max, I think you should try and move on," I say, copying his movements.

"Why?"

"Because," I almost whine. "What we have... it's too strong. I love you too much it hurts, it hurts to be away from you. It felt like my heart was being ripped out of my chest when you 'cheated' on me. This... it's not right."

Max takes a step back, hurt on his face. "What's wrong with it being too strong? It shows how real this is."

Running a hand through my hair, I chew on my lip. "You're not hearing me."

Max cocks an eyebrow. "Oh, I'm not?"

"I knew you wouldn't be okay with this deal." I accuse, jabbing a finger in his direction. He lied to me!

Max huffs, stomping over to me. "I am and I'm not. There! There's the truth. I want to respect your decision, I really do because that's what people do when they are in love. But I also want to hate you for basically making my decision for me. Asking to make me wait for you is selfish. But a part of me wants to wait because it's you."

My heart stops.

"But maybe you are right. Maybe we need to distance ourselves and work out where we need to go."

I gaze into his brown eyes, searching them for dishonesty. When I see nothing of the sort, a sense of relief flows through me.

"If you are going to discover yourself - so am I. I have spent the past two years wallowing in grief, dead. But now, now is my chance to find myself again too. It appears we are both going on a hunt for each other."

"Yes," I reply, smiling slightly. "It appears we are."

"You know, I'm proud of you. You finally put yourself first and thought about what you need." Max utters, bringing a finger up to my face. Slowly, like he's memorizing the action, he drags it down my cheek. His finger leaves a trail of sparks, sparks that I will never forget.

"You're the same. You are the dream guy - you know that?" I whisper, maintaining eye contact with him. "Any girl will be lucky to date you."

"Well, Ava, in case things don't work out between us, whilst we are alone, I want to tell you it has been a pleasure. We have made some amazing memories, we've had our mistakes but we are learning from them. I will always remember you." Max says, putting his hands on my shoulders.

I feel sad at his words, knowing that it could be true. We may never act the same again, after this day, I will begin my search as will he. He may meet a new girl.

I am going to be happy for him no matter what. Whether I don't see him anymore or if I do.

"Max, you will always have a special place in my heart. You will always be my first love, my first kiss, my first everything. I hope that if we do drift apart, that our paths will cross one day." I tell him, insuinating that if he doesn't see me on graduation day, that we would meet up.

Max smiles. "I'm sure they will."

Max then closes the distance between us and pecks my lips, possibly for the last time. My eyes flutter shut and enjoy the blissful moment. I will always remember his lips against mine.

"Now, do you want to go in the sea?" He asks me and I quickly nod my head, the corners of my lips quirking upwards. "You better run than otherwise, I'll catch you."

With a squeal, I sprint off, laughing all the way to the sea.

26

26 | The Troubles With Bree

Max and I made it back to LA just in time for the dinner. We both stumbled into the restaurant, apologizing to our parents who only gave us amused looks. Its been no secret that my parents always liked us together. Many times they have hinted for us to marry.

They were absolutely shocked when we split. My mother especially, who demanded to know what was wrong. When I refused to tell her, she practically begged me to give Max a second chance.

"So, where did you two go?" Max's mom, Callie, asked. She is an awfully sweet lady, who always had a smile on her face. Her brown eyes, that Max also has, twinkle in delight.

"To the beach," I answer, smiling.

Callie then flings her arms around me from her seat next to me. Briefly, I close my eyes and melt in her sweet, cinnamon scent. Callie is one of the many things I missed when I left Max.

"How are you, sweetie?" She murmurs.

Smiling when Callie pulls away, I answer her. "Alright. I missed you though."

Callie puts a hand on her heart, giving me a flattering look. "I'm touched Ava, I really am. I knew I loved you for a reason."

I laugh loudly at that, throwing my head back. Max catches my eye, noticing my enthusiasm. He stops his conversation with my parents and simply stares at me. Events like this were something we used to love. It bonded us closer together, strengthen our relationship.

"How's school going Ava?" Max's dad, Julian, asks me with interest.

And so that's how the evening goes - with me catching up with Max's parents and him doing the same with our parents. After we ate the delicious and divine meal, Max and I leave, letting our parents catch up more and make arrangements for the future. Max leads me to his car and politely opens his door, mock bowing. I laugh, rolling my eyes.

The car journey, once again, is spent with us singing and bouncing in our seats to songs.

Eventually, Max pulls up to my house. I suck in a breath and stare at it for a second. This could be the last time Max and I have a moment like this. Everything is going to change - I can feel it. I'm terrified that I will never see him again, I will never have moments like this again but I'm also excited about the future. The very prospect of graduating is chillingly extravagant.

I turn my face back to Max, observing him. His face, his eyes, say the same as mine does. But we both know, we both realized, that we have our lives ahead of us and we need to discover things alone.

Suddenly, I hug Max. His arms instantly wrap around my form, bringing me closer to him. I nestle my head into his neck and breathe in his masculine scent. Max tightens his grip on me when he realizes what I'm doing.

Reluctantly, I pull away from him. My body yearns for his but I ignore it. Instead, I listen to that rational voice in my head. My right-hand moves to the door handle, whilst I stay focused on Max. We stare at each other like this is our last meeting, that this is our last time together.

"You're amazing. Remember that." I say and get out of the car, lifting my bag up in the process. Slamming the door shut, I march up to my house, feeling his eyes on me.

I don't turn back.

On Monday, the first day of Max and I was separated but were still close to each other, I searched for Bree. Its about time the mess with Harry was sorted. Bree is slowly beginning to worm her way into my heart;

the very thought of her hurt makes me mad to no end. So I want to help her sort things out with Harry.

I finally managed to locate Bree, in the bathrooms. Walking in, I stand next to her, facing the mirror. My face - my blue eyes, pale, heart-shaped face stares back at me. Once upon a time, not too long ago, I found myself very insecure about how I looked. I still do - we all do. But knowing I can be loved not only by my looks but my personality, gives me a boost of confidence.

"I've been looking everywhere for you," I say, watching her fix her hair through the mirror.

Bree's green eyes flicker to mine through the mirror, with a hint of nervousness and then they move back to her own reflection. She weaves her fingers through her red locks, letting her curls bounce when she's finished.

"And I was looking for you," Bree replies.

I blink. "What?"

Bree rolls her eyes and turns to face me, putting her hand on the counter. "At the party. Last I remember, Molly got wasted and you went off. I think I caught you kissing some guy and then letting Max lead you up to a room but that's it. You totally ditched me."

My mouth opens in understanding and I flash her a sympathetic smile. I completely forgot about Bree at the party. I got so upset with myself that I didn't think about who was looking after her. I just assumed that since the boys were looking after Molly, they would look after her too.

"Oh gosh, I'm so sorry. I was so wasted, I literally had a break down in front of Max." I rush out. "I hope you were alright. And I hope you can forgive me."

Bree scrutinizes me for a second, enjoying the fact that I'm feeling guilty. Maybe this is her way of teaching me a lesson. I have been a bad friend lately. I have been prioritizing Max. But now I'm going to focus more on my friends. I'm going to help Bree with Harry and I'm going to get Molly to open up more. She's an amazing person and she needs to see it.

"Of course I can forgive you." She finally says and pulls me in for a hug. "Just don't ditch me again."

"Never," I whisper into her ear, squeezing her shoulders.

The bell rings loudly, announcing the start of lessons. Groaning, I trudge my way to my first lesson with Molly. I can't believe its Monday - the worst day of the week.

***

At lunch today, the group notices a shift in the atmosphere. And I'm not just meaning because Harry and Bree are glaring at each other but because Max isn't here. None of picked up the courage to ask me yet but I know they are all dying to.

I think Luke has worked it out because he whispered to Lawrence: "I think she's back in the market."

He received a slap on the head for that.

"Okay, where on earth is Max?" Josh is the first to ask the question. He avoids looking in Bree and Harry's direction, sensing some sort of sexual tension. The two of them were good at hiding it for a while but now it's just obvious.

Sighing, I dump my fork in my salad. "Max and I have come to an agreement. Not that friendship agreement but a new one. We both know that we need time to enjoy ourselves this year and focus on studying. He needs to find out what he wants like I do so we are...well...having a break from the friendship."

Nobody says a word. I had expected this though.

"And how are you feeling about this?" Molly asks me, in a soft tone. She gives me a warm smile and slings a reassuring arm over my shoulder. I admit, having the moral support feels nice.

I wonder how Rosie would react to the news...if only she would talk to me.

"I'm okay with it. We both agreed to it. Perhaps this is for the best. Not everyone's first love is their true love." I answer, noting how Bree and Harry both shuffle in their seats at my words.

Molly nods her head, seeing my point of view. Lawrence smiles, Luke gives me his trademark smirk and Josh bumps my shoulder.

"Now that that's sorted." Lawrence clears his throat and turns to the two people at the end of our table. "What is going on with you two?"

Harry and Bree both snap their necks to Lawrence, their eyes widening. They both look like two deers caught in headlights.

"Oh - uh." Bree splutters. To try and distract all of the attention from her, she begins brushing her hair behind her ear whilst giving Harry pointed looks. Poor Harry looks clueless on where to start or what to say.

"So what exactly happened at that party last Friday?" I ask, saving the two of them from embarrassment. Taking the bait, Luke begins to reiterate the night - well, his experience of the night.

Whilst pretending to listen to him, I give Bree a wink when she sends me a thankful look.

After lunch, I walk with Bree to her next lesson, hoping she will update me on her and Harry. A massive part of me wants them to just admit that they love each other and get together. But that would be hypocritical of me.

I now know it's not as simple as that.

I honestly thought the two of them were working things out but at the last minute, Bree changed her mind. So nothing between them has changed.

"Do you know what I think you two should do?" I ask, swinging my arms back and forth. At one point, I accidentally hit a boy. Whilst apologizing, he gives me a scowl and marches off. Oops? Bree gives me a side glance, encouraging me to continue. "Talk to him!"

It's the most logical and most obvious thing to do. Bree is scared - I understand that. But she needs to face her fears and talk to him. Sitting down, having a coffee, talking about their fears will mean they can solve all of their problems.

"I -I" She stutters. "I -"

"Yeah, no." I interrupt her. "Talking to Max basically cleared up everything. We both know what we have to do now. Just do it."

Bree clamps her mouth shut and spins on her heel, off to find Harry.

27

27 | Moving On

"He totally asked you out," Bree says, spinning her spoon around in her cup. Molly rolls her eyes, completely unconvinced. "Don't deny it. What you just said literally described a guy nervously asking a girl he likes out."

"But I heard he was trouble!" Molly exclaims, a bit too loud. She receives a few dirty looks from some older people. Grace, the owner of our now regular coffee show, sends a glance our way. Molly sinks in her chair, embarrassed by the amount of attention she's suddenly getting.

"All the best ones are." Bree sends her a wink. I pinch my lips together to stop myself from laughing at Molly's reaction. She can be quite adorable sometimes.

"That's it! Can we move on now?" Molly asks, with a hint of desperation in her voice. I understand why she wants to leave the subject where it is - talking about her own boy troubles can be a scary thing for people who are more reserved, who have never experienced anything like it before. I remember when I first got into a relationship with Max - I was freaking terrified of everything. Everything was new, different.

Molly had reiterated to us her experience with some guy who claimed he liked her. She seems scared of accepting his date because of his reputation. Apparently, he doesn't have the best image for dating girls.

Reluctantly, Bree leans back into her chair and shuts her mouth.

A comfortable silence settles between us. Molly looks deep in thought, with her eyebrows furrowed and her lips slightly apart. Bree appears to have found amusement in watching two toddlers fight whilst I watch a young couple.

The two teenagers look like they are sixteen, maybe seventeen. By their awkward, closed body language, I'm assuming this is their first date. Whilst they look uncomfortable, I can see the love in their eyes.

The boy murmurs something to the girl, eagerly awaiting her answer. When she replies, I notice how he hangs off every single word she says. It's the sweetest thing I have seen.

Once upon a time, I had a guy like that. Things happened between us and we realized that before getting together, we need to discover ourselves. Going our different ways is a great idea. I need time where I need to focus on myself and not a boy. I need to find out what I want. Even if he's what I want.

He needs to do the same. He needs to decide what he wants.

What a true story. In reality, most things don't end up like a Disney story where the princess falls in love with the prince and they live happily ever after. This is the real world, not the cartoon world.

And I'm happy with my decision. Well, almost happy. A part of me is still nagging, pushing me the other way. The way back to Max. But I did the right thing.

"You okay there?" Molly asks me, gazing at the couple I'm looking at and then me. Her dark brown eyes show worry in them - for me.

I blink. "Yeah."

"Are you sure about that?" She arches an eyebrow.

"I am. I was just lost in thought." I tell her, hopefully convincing her that I'm telling the truth.

Molly gives me a skeptical look. Ever since I declared Max and I are going to...distance ourselves from each other, Molly has been by my shoulder, waiting for me to break down. As flattering as it is to know she's ready to be there for me, I also feel a tad bit hurt that she doesn't believe I'm strong enough to get over this.

Because I am. I know that now.

I'm strong enough to be selfless and put Max's needs before my own. He may have wanted me but he didn't need me. If he does, I will find out next year.

"Hmm," she says. "I'm proud of you. I hope you know that. You basically set Max free. Which is so brave and kind. You are amazing. Know that."

"Aww, thanks," I say, my eyes welling up.

This is when Bree bounces back to our world. "Yeah, what you did was inspiring. So inspiring that I went up to Harry and told him we have to talk about everything that happened between us. We are meeting here after school tomorrow."

"That's amazing!" I nearly yell, recalling what happened a couple of minutes ago with Molly. Springing out of my seat, I move around the small coffee table and give Bree a hug. Damn, it would have been so easier if she had sat on the sofa next to me.

"Alright, alright." She laughs, wrapping her arms around me. "Don't squeeze me to death otherwise I will never talk to him."

All three of us laugh at that and continue to drink our delicious drinks.

***

A few days pass after our coffee trip. Bree met up with Harry and talked about everything. Bree told me they discussed everything for hours and came to a decision. I was so happy when she said they were going to give it another go but a lot slower.

The guys found out about everything and were completely shocked. Typical that they couldn't work out there was something going on between them. Even when Bree and Harry were sharing intense looks, they couldn't put the pieces together.

Molly also admitted she accepted the date. It's actually tonight. She's a bit nervous but with some encouragement from Bree and me, she feels a bit better. When Josh found out, he flipped.

Molly told us that it took her two hours to convince him to let her go.

I laughed at that.

The bell had just rung, meaning everybody is going home, to enjoy the weekend. The gang and I decided we are going to go paintballing tomorrow. I'm actually really excited to go since I've never been before.

Bree did inform me earlier that it really hurts, especially if you get hit up close. I gulped at that and pretended I didn't hear it.

I practically skip to my car, with a gleeful expression on my face. Giving the guys a wave, I open my car door.

As I dump my bag in the passenger seat, I notice a certain somebody also opening their door. Max, who looks just as gorgeous as he always does, glances up at me as if sensing I'm looking at him.

Our eyes lock. We stare for a few seconds and then I break it, for a moment. I haven't spoken to Max since last week. I've seen him in the halls, chatting with his friends. In class, he does his work instead of disturbing me. Its as if we are strangers. He's sometimes talking to one of the guys. Since he doesn't sit with us anymore, he tends to talk to them in P.E. or outside of school when I'm not there. I'm happy he's still keeping in contact with them. I wouldn't want to be the reason they stopped talking.

But that's alright. Sure, I miss him like crazy. But I'm also pleased with myself and him. We are doing the right thing for the both of us.

I smile and give him a wave. He does the same and gets in his car. And I do the same, that longing pressing harder on my heart.

***

"Just remember, once you've been hit by the opposite team, you are out." Lawrence reminds us, readjusting his vest top. I nod my head, glancing at Bree with a mischevious look.

The teams were randomly selected by the employees here. Josh, Harry, Molly and I are on one team whilst Bree, Lawrence and Luke are on another team. Lawrence recently told me he does this all the time and is really good at it.

So now that he's on the other team, I'm a bit scared.

The game is capture the flag. The team who gets the flag first wins. Simple, right?

God, no.

About five minutes into the game, I'm panting. My legs are aching, protesting that they don't want to run anymore. But I continue.

Molly, being the least sporty person here (shocking, I know), was hit about thirty seconds into the game. So that means the teams are even and I'm their next target. They always go for the weak ones first.

Josh and Harry had run off as soon as the whistle was blown. I didn't catch where the other teams were. So, as soon as Molly was hit, I ran.

And I've been running since. I have no clue where the white flag is but I'm hoping its close and unguarded.

But alas, life isn't as easy as pie. Of course, I end up finding one of the opposite team. And of course, it has to be the one person who knows this game better than anyone else - Lawrence.

"Congratulations Ava, you are the third person to be out." He says and shoots me. My poor chest feels the force of the blow; I nearly double over. Thankfully, the pain disappears as quickly as it arrived.

Bree wasn't kidding. Now I'm going to have a bruise on my chest. Wonderful.

"At least I wasn't the first," I tell Lawrence and he laughs, sprinting off somewhere else. That's when I begin to trudge my way back to base, passing a very excited Luke on the way.

28

28 | I Made A Mistake

"Thanks, Ava. What you did was amazing." Miranda says, her voice laced with gratitude. Smiling, I take my apron off and head over to the locker room.

My forehead is sweating from all of the work I was doing in the hot conditions. I wipe it off with the back of my hand, releasing a tired sigh.

"Hey Ava," Katilyn pops her head around the corner. "This was left for you."

She hands me a small piece of paper. Curiously, I accept it and wish Katilyn thanks. After joining this homeless shelter, I met Katilyn who is a really nice person. She has been working here for three years, ever since her aunt admitted she was homeless to her family. She said she wanted to help everyone else who was in the same position as her aunt out.

Me, I wanted to join because I needed a distraction. Its nearly been a whole school year and with my exams almost over, I have more time. I started here a few months ago; have loved every moment here.

I also decided to do this to take my mind off of Max. It has been a lot harder than I expected for me to do things my own way. Perhaps if I was somewhere away from him, I would find it easier. But seeing him at least four times a week has been challenging.

I haven't heard much from him. I think I overheard some girl gossiping that he was going on a date with someone my age. Apparently, she was a cheerleader. At first, I felt a tidal wave of jealousy. I had pictured that he would be ready to ask me the question as soon as graduation day came. But after a lot of mental deliberation, I came to realize that I shouldn't be angry with him or jealous. This was my choice. And as a friend, I should be happy for him.

Never sad, angry or jealous.

And so I sucked it up. I plastered a smile on my face and felt happy for him. And I do. This is his choice, it's his life.

We both needed time away from each other. We both needed to find ourselves and what we wanted. For too long, we let that incident determine our lives. But not anymore.

"Thanks, Katilyn," I say with a smile. She returns it and then disappears again, back to work.

My fingers skim the thin piece of paper, wondering what it could say and who it could be from. If it's from George, one of the workers who has been set on dating me since the moment I arrived, I'm going to kill him.

Mentally, I shake my head from those thoughts and unfold the note. As soon as I see my name written, I note how it isn't in Geroge's handwriting but in someone else's - an unfamiliar handwriting.

Ava,

I'm sorry I couldn't say this to you in person. I know I would prefer it would be better with spoken words. So I apologize.

I am writing this letter to thank you for all of the work you have done for me. When I first came here, I was miserable and lonely. I couldn't see a future for myself. But you encouraged me to pursue my happiness. For someone so young, you are very wise. Every Sunday, I looked forward to your shift, ready to hear one of your funny stories or your little pep talks. Because o those talks, I am going to be starting a new job next week.

I never would have gotten to where I am without you. You put faith in me, hope. And I will always be in debt to you for that.

I have also noticed how sad you look. I'm not completely familiar with what's going on in your life but if I could take a guess, from experience, I would say you are lost. Heartbroken. Lonely. So I'm going to give you the exact same advice you gave me. Pursue your happiness, Ava. Because you deserve it too.

You may think you are doing the right thing for yourself or others but you may not be. Don't dwell on that now, you are young, live in the moment. Whoever the man you lost is, must be incredibly special. And you must have loved him deeply. For once, follow your heart. Do something for yourself.

With lots of love,

Karen XX

P.S. if you do come to your senses and follow your heart, remember to take that brain with you.

I laugh at the last part of her note, imagining her grinning ear to ear whilst writing that.

Tears stream down my face. Not tears of sadness but tears of joy, happiness. Never have I received such an emotional letter before.

Karen really got to me there. I am so pleased that she got a new job. She has been unemployed for a long time now. Knowing that my encouragement got her to try again is the best feeling in the world. It's indescribable.

Her words towards me, concerning Max, who she never knew about makes me second guess my decision. I thought I made the right decision, for the both of us. We both needed to find ourselves. I wanted us to focus solely on our studies and careers. Feelings were an afterthought.

But now...what if that was it? What if our moment together is officially over?

Honestly, I don't want it to be. I want him to be mine forever. I love him. Time won't change that, a new girl won't change that. I can't change that.

Maybe I shouldn't worry about school. I know where I'm going, long distance can be a thing. Whenever love is concerned, you always fight for it. We can fight. I know Max can - he's been fighting for it the moment I stepped into the school. Me? I've been fighting against it.

I know what I want to be. I know what I want. And I know we can make it work.

Graduation is next week. On that day, I'm going to be waiting for him. And if he doesn't come to me, I'll come to him. I'll show him I'm fighting for us now, that I want him. He at least deserves to know that I'm committed and that I know I'm an idiot.

A complete idiot.

***

"I made a mistake," I state, matter of factly to the girls who are both lying casually on my bed.

Molly bolts upright, catching onto what I mean. Bree frowns in confusion.

"What?" She murmurs, perplexed.

I roll my eyes. "With Max," I answer her. "I thought we should split apart to help us find ourselves. I thought we could test to see if we need each other. But I only freaking realized that I always did, even when I thought I hated him. I already know who I am, so does he. I found myself when I was with him, I was the person I wanted to be. School work can't break us up, I can."

With a breath, I continue. "I have to tell him on graduation day, no matter what his reaction is. He needs to know I'm willing to do this, that I know I want him. He's the man for me, no one can compare. He's what I need in my life. I love him."

Bree sits up too, with a stunned expression. My attention turns to Molly who is grinning like a Cheshire cat.

"Yes!" She squeals, hopping off of the bed. She starts doing a mini dance, her dark brown curls bouncing up and down on her back. "Finally! I didn't want to interfere because you needed to work it out for yourself. And now, finally, you see that he was good for you. He wasn't a distraction, an interference, he was a supportive shoulder, a magnet to put you straight again. Thank god, you finally saw it. I was starting to worry that the wake-up call wasn't going to happen."

With an agape mouth, I stare at Molly with wide eyes. What the hell was that?

"U - uh," Bree stutters, eyeing Molly cautiously. With her gleaming eyes, wide smile and flustered cheeks, anyone would think she had just won the lottery. "Are you okay Molly?"

Molly frantically nods her head, "I'm fine now."

Bree purses her lips together but doesn't delve deeper.

"But I'm so glad you finally woke up! Now you can go after your man." Molly adds, smiling brightly. "Aren't you Bree? We've all seen how she hasn't been the same since they split. Now she can be happy again."

"You're right," Bree agrees, "I'm glad you are going to do the right thing." She then pauses. "So what are you going to do to get him back?"

And so I proceed to tell them my plan. I also admit how afraid I am of rejection. It has been months since we've had an encounter and for all I know, he could still be dating that girl. I really haven't been paying attention to gossip. But I won't let that stop me from at least speaking my thoughts - feelings.

Because Max deserves to know every single one of them.

"I really hope you guys get back together," Molly says.

"They are perfect together," Bree adds.

I smile at the pair of them and bring them in for a hug. What did I do to get such amazing friends?

29

29 | The Plan

If you're wondering about Rosie, I will tell you. I waited for her to talk to me for months. I hoped and prayed she would finally back down and talk to me. Rosie has always been a stubborn person, just like me. She didn't like to be the first person to apologize. It hurt her pride.

It was the 22nd of December when I received my first message from her in a long time. I can remember it well. I was wrapping presents for everybody whilst listening to Christmas music when she sent me a text message. At first, I was so shocked she messaged me that I thought I was in a dream.

But then I pinched myself.

After discovering how real the text was, I was quick to reply. I didn't feel anger towards her. No, I was past that by now. I had gone so long without her craziness I just missed her.

So when she called me, I started crying. Turns out Rosie was feeling the exact same way. She was bawling her eyes out on the other side of the line, sobbing about how much she missed me and much of a jerk she was. For hours we talked about everything. I told her everything about Max and she told me how sorry she was for abruptly ending the call like that and then for ignoring me.

It was three in the morning when I finally finished my call with her. Not that I regretted staying up late though. I finally had my best friend back. Albeit, we still have a few things to discuss but we were getting there.

Now, with graduation tomorrow, I am so happy Rosie is here with me. Her graduation was two days ago so she hopped on the first coach to here. When I saw her in person, I cried. The whole of yesterday was spent with the both of us having fun and talking about Max. Now she realized her mistake, she is going to be more supportive of my decision. I know she isn't happy with it but she doesn't want to lose me.

Yesterday, I introduced Bree and Molly to her. Luckily, they all get along with each other. The girls and I chilled with Netflix and talked about Prom. Just thinking about it makes me want to burst out into fits of laughter.

Of course, Luke snuck alcohol into the school. As you can imagine, he got absolutely wasted. Josh wasn't too bad, partly because he was watching over Molly and her date. Bree and Harry were with each other the whole time, snuggling up with each other and snogging. A lot. And then Luke kept flirting with other girls, drunk, whilst his date had an arm around his. I felt so sorry for the poor girl. She didn't deserve to be disrespected like that.

Lawrence, Josh and I were the only ones without dates. Not that I minded. When the couples went off to dance, we would join up as a three and dance. I didn't care that I didn't have a date. It was fun with the boys.

After prom finished, a few of us went to the after party. Reluctantly, Josh took Luke home. Molly and her date went to the party by themselves; Harry and Bree went with Lawrence and me.

I didn't stay that long though. Prom had taken a lot out of me.

And no, I didn't see Max at prom. I assumed he was either ill that day or he was never in the area I was in. Sometimes, I do wonder whether he went with his football friends or with a date - specifically that girl.

All in all, though, it was an incredible night. I made many memories that I will look back on with a laugh.

***

"So which university did you end up choosing, Molly?" Rosie asks her, flopping down on my bed. Molly, who is spinning in my spinny chair, stops moving.

"Brown."

Rosie's eyebrows raised in shock as if Molly had just told her she was related to the president. Which she could be...you never know.

"What about you Ava?" She turns her attention to me, with a curious expression on her face.

"I didn't apply," I answer truthfully. I didn't apply for many reasons, one being that I didn't know what I wanted to do. The more time I spent volunteering, the more I began to realize how much I enjoyed it. That letter from Karen meant so much to me. The fact I helped somebody out and turned their world upside down, from something dark to light, changes you.

And another reason, that I won't admit aloud, is Max.

They all lift their eyebrows in surprise, obviously not expecting me to do something like that. Their reaction is similar to my parents but it's not as dramatic.

"So what are you planning to do?" Bree asks me.

"Well," I sigh, twirling a strand of my hair around my finger. "I was looking online at volunteering programmes in places like Africa and thought maybe, I could go there."

"That sounds amazing," Molly smiles.

I nod my head, smiling. Helping people in need is something I have to do. I want to be a better person after everything I did with Max and this will not only help me do that but will open up my mind.

We then start to talk about graduation and what we think it will be like. We're all nervous about it because it's our last time in high school.

This past year has been a whirlwind of emotions but I'm glad it happened.

I'm not glad I ended things with Max. I know its so selfish to hope he will get back with me but I know I have to at least try. Then, in the future, I can't say I didn't try.

"Ava, what's the plan for tomorrow then?"

I purse my lips at her question. In all honesty, my plan isn't extravagant or big. I was planning just to go up to him and tell him how I felt. It would be awkward if I did something flashy and big in front of everyone only to be rejected.

"You're going to go up and talk to him aren't you?" Rosie says my answer aloud.

I nod my head.

"Right then," Rosie clucks her tongue. "We need to come up with a better plan. It's time you whooed him off of his feet."

"What are you thinking Rosie?" Bree eyes her with suspicion. Rosie's eyes sparkle with mischief and excitement.

"I'm thinking...we need to go to the grocery store," Rosie answers, cryptically.

The three of us exchange confused looks but get up when she does and follow her. I am curious about what she has planned.

30

30 | I Love You

Graduation was so sad yet so exciting. I had shed a few tears at the speeches given and whenever I thought about how I wasn't going to see walk down the school halls again. The thought that I would never eat in the dining hall again or listen to high school drama was paining.

After we threw our hats in the air, I searched the area for Max. But, of course, I couldn't find him. Rosie has this extravagant plan of having me sing--which I can't even do--a song. She got the idea from the film Walking On Sunshine where the main character sang If I Could Turn Back Time by Cher. As romantic as it sounds, I honestly have my doubts. For starters, I can't sing so I'm going to make a fool of myself. Secondly, Max could completely disregard me.

I mean, if he sees I'm willing to embarrass myself for him, he might at least let me explain myself. But I'm completely forgetting about that girl he could be with. If he really likes her, there's no way he will leave her for me. I mess things up and I let him go

"Do you see him?" Bree comes up and asks me. I shake my head in disappointment. She squeezes my shoulders in comfort and gives me a small smile. "Don't worry, I'm sure he'll turn up soon."

I'm not.

"Group photo!" Molly shouts from behind me, drawing my attention to her. The rest of the group appear, along with Rosie and we all pose for a photograph. I smile, hoping nobody notices its fake. "Let's do one with silly faces!" She suggests and starts bouncing up and down in excitement. Rolling my eyes at her antics, I smile, for real and do as she says, pulling a funny face.

We pose for a few more photos and paired photos. Tiredness begins to overwash me. Who knew taking so many photos would tire one out so much?

My parents come back over to me, holding their little camera and take a few photos and then they leave, knowing I want to spend some time with my friends alone. I think I catch Max's parents at one point during the time but before I could pinpoint them, they had vanished.

"Guys, I'm going to dump my things in my car, I'll meet you there in a few," I inform them once we've finished taking pictures. We had planned to go out to the diner to get food and then, hopefully, we would go to Lawrence's house.

They nod their heads and I run over to where my car is parked. Slightly out of breath, I reach my car and unlock it, throwing everything in the back seat.

Finished, I turn around and stumble into a body. Muscular arms wrap around me, preventing me from falling. A familiar, musky scent fills my nose and jogs my memory. I could never forget that smell. His smell.

I peak up at his face through my eyelashes, my heart banging in my chest at the sight of his gorgeous brown eyes.

I feel as if I've been deprived of Max's eyes for so long. It's weird but true. I missed the way they stared at me, the way they would soften. I missed letting him hold me, keep me safe from everything. God, I missed him.

Max's eyes search my face, especially my eyes. When he sees something, though I have no clue what, he gives me a breathtaking smile. That smile that gives me goosebumps and has me wanting more.

"M--Max," I breathe out, nervously yet cheerfully. He's here! He's here right now and I didn't have to hunt him down. He found me.

"Ava," he replies smoothly.

"I--I was looking for you," I tell him, maintaining eye contact with him.

His eyes light up, "really?"

I nod my head quickly, "yeah, I have something to say to you."

"I have something to say to you as well," he declares. "You first."

Okay, I can do this. I have been waiting a while for this and there is no way I'm going to do something stupid like chicken out. I want to be with Max and I have to tell him how much he means to me. How I really want to be with him.

How I love him.

Because god, I love him. So, so much.

I flutter my eyes closed for a second and take a deep breath. I have got this. I can do this.

"Max, a few months ago I made the biggest mistake of my life. I let you go. At the time, I thought I was doing the right thing for the both of us but I was wrong. I was so wrong. I guess that quote 'you don't know what you have until you lose it' rings perfectly for this situation because the moment I lost you was the moment I realized I loved you too much to let you go. I want you to know that I love you and I know I'm a complete idiot but I hope you would possibly...I dunno...give us a second or even third chance." I say from the bottom of my heart.

I peer back up at him, praying he'll really consider my words.

Max is silent for a few moments.

With bated breath, I wait for him to say anything.

"Well," he eventually says, evenly. "I was hoping you would say that. I have something to say too."

I hold my breath.

"These past few months have been eye-opening for me too." He starts. "I'm so in love and I knew I had to let the girl know so I could be with her."

Oh god, oh god. What is happening? What if he's on about that other girl and he has to tell me this so I don't interfere. Oh no. Oh no.

My eyes widen in panic and begin to water. I swallow the lump forming in my throat and try to stay calm.

But the thought: I'm too late keeps reoccurring in my head.

"So that's why I'm here. I have to tell her that I do love her, even if she doesn't want to be with me." I want to cry. "But, then she said it first, she told me how much she hated being apart and how sorry she was. When she told me how much she loved me, I felt everything fall into place."

Hold on...

"Yes Sunshine, I'm talking about you."

I sigh in relief. I don't know what I would have done if he was in love with another girl. I think I would have gone home and cried for weeks.

I leap onto him, wrapping my arms around his neck, catching him by surprise.

Max chuckles and slowly spins me around. Giggles erupt from my throat as I feel happiness course through me.

"I love you so much," I whisper into his ear. "I'm so sorry that I wanted to wait. It was so stupid."Max shakes his head and meets me dead in the eye. "It wasn't. You needed to know what you wanted and now you do."

I guess. If I hadn't, I doubt I would have done volunteering.

"Should we go somewhere?" Max suggests and wiggles his eyebrows. I smack him for his dirty mind, laughing lightly. Already, having Max back with me is truly incredible.

"Oh, the gang and I are going to a diner. Do you want to join us?" I ask him, nibbling on my bottom lip.

His eyes darken at my action and he stiffly nods his head.

Max gets into my car, telling me that he left his car at home because he parents brought him here. The car ride isn't awkward in the slightest and we catch up on what we missed in each other's lives.

During the ride, I asked the one question I was dying to know. "Max, what--what about that girl you were with? Aren't you dating her?"

Max turns to face me with a smirk. His eyes glimmer with mischief and amusement. Dammit, he's finding this funny.

"You jealous sunshine?" He questions. I turn my head to face the road, knowing that if I continue to stare into his brown orbs, I will get lost in them. And that will lead to us having a car crash. Since I'm not looking directly at him, I play it off like its nothing. "Pfft, no. I don't get jealous."Beside me, Max chuckles.

"I think you are." He states. "But don't worry, I wasn't dating a girl."

"W--What?" I splutter with wide eyes. "But there were rumors! P--People said you were with a girl."

I glance at Max. He raises an eyebrow at me. "And you believe rumors? Since when?"Okay, he has a point. The other day, people said that the deputy headteacher was actually a secret spy since she recently had lots of security cameras installed. It's crazy what people can come up with.

"True, I just...I thought you would because you wanted to move on," I admit, sheepishly. Max laughs and for the rest of the journey, we tease each other and make jokes.

The diner is buzzing with celebratory teenagers when we arrive. I easily spot the gang and head over to them, with Max's hand in mine.

Molly is the first to spot us.

"Oh. My. Gosh." She squeals and get's the rest of the group's attention. "Look!"

Rosie and Bree smirk and the boys give us shocked expressions.

"I knew that song would work," Rosie says. Max frowns and gives me a 'what?' look. I shake my head and mouth 'tell you later' to him.

"So...are you two back together?" Josh asks us, grinning.

"Yep buddy," Max answers and then proceeds to do the bro hug thing with Josh. All of us girls share a look and shake our heads.

Boys

We spend a good hour chatting away, annoying the workers here with our loud conversations. But hey, we're celebrating. School's over

"So...party?" Lawrence brings up the possible plan for later. Despite it still being early, having some fun as a group at Lawrence's seems like a good idea.

We all nod, smiling. Party sounds good.

"Do you want to go to the party for a bit and then go somewhere together?" Max whispers into my ear as we leave the diner.

"Yeah," I mutter back, internally squealing.

After making a brief appearance at Lawrence's house, Max and I leave. I give him the keys to the car, fed up of listening to his pleads for me to give it to him.

Thirty minutes later, Max drives off of the road and onto a small road leading to god knows where.

He parks on grass and turns his head to me. I'm too busy staring straight ahead at the sea to look at him though. The sight of the bright blue sky and the blazing sun is blissful. I get out of the car and take a photo.

"Thank you for bringing me here," I tell Max, sincerely.

"Anytime," Max replies and comes around the car, standing behind me. He wraps his arms around me and brings my back to his chest whilst resting his chin on the top of my head. This moment is perfect.

"Wait," I say suddenly remembering something else I need to ask. "Last year, you had a surprise for me but it never happened in the end. I have to know, what was it?"

Max thinks for a moment and then smiles. "Oh yes, that. I had convinced Rosie to come and apologize but she never showed up in the end. After I messaged her but she never replied. I don't know why she didn't come through. Maybe you could try asking her? I heard you two are friends again."

Wow, even after everything, Max was still thinking about me.

"I love you," I blurt out without hesitation.

Max gives me his beautiful smile. "I love you too sunshine."

31 | The End

"No, no no!" I argue, shaking my head. There is no way he's going to make me do this! No way in hell.

Max pouts, pecking my lips. "Please," he begs. "For me."

Goddammit, he can't make that face. The cute one where he widens his eyes and puckers his lips. The way he's looking at me, it's not even fair. I can't say no to that face and he knows it.

"Max, stop it." I snap, stepping back. I glance back up at the ride, gulping at the number of twists and turns. The people on the carriage scream in terror. Yeah, there's no way I'm going on that.

Max follows my line of sight and smirks. "Stop doing what? I'm not doing anything. I'm just a boyfriend begging his girlfriend to join him on the ride."

My insides nearly melt when he says 'girlfriend', referring to me. Even after getting back with him a month ago, I still can't believe it. These past few weeks have been amazing. Since its the summer holidays, we have been trying to do as much as we can. We went to the beach the other day and we went on a date. Today, we invited the group on an overnight trip to Universal Orlando Studios.

Now I'm regretting it because Max wants me to go on the scariest ride here. I'm not a massive fan of rollercoasters. I have Acrophobia--a fear of heights.

"Max, you know I can't...handle those rides," I say, with a shaky voice. "Just ask Josh or Lawrence to go on with you."

Max stares into my eyes and sighs. "Fine," he says and runs a hand through his hair. "I'll just ask one of the guys."

With a triumphant smile, I watch him head off to find them. When he's out of sight, I turn around and search for the girls.

Then, suddenly, hands wrap around my waist and lift me up in the air. I scream in surprise and kick my legs. When I hear that husky chuckle, the one that sends shivers down my spine, I know exactly who is holding me.

Max.

"Are you serious?" I ask rhetorically. Max puts me down and spins me around, only to lift me up again and put me on his shoulder. My face stares at his back whilst my legs are in perfect sight for Max to see. Along with my butt. Wonderful.

Max chuckles when I attempt to slap the back of his head. I'm in an awkward position so it's a lot harder to twist my torso around and slap him on the head. I scowl and stop struggling. As long as he puts me down soon and doesn't take me to that ride, everything will be fine.

***

Everything is not fine. I'm about to be strapped up on the ride. Max had dropped me in the line with him and spent the entire time waiting in the line persuading me to get on it. After lots of begging and kisses, I relented. And now, as I'm about to get on the ride, I'm regretting it. Why did I listen to Max?

Fear is etched on my face. My hands tremble beside me and a lump has formed in my throat. I'm going to be screaming the entire time--I know it.

"Don't worry Sunshine, if you fall, I'll be falling with you," Max whispers into my ear and chuckles.

I slap his chest. "Not funny." I snap and take a shaky breath. The worker gestures to two seats and Max happily gets into the one furthest away. Slowly, I follow him. The man lowers the bar and checks how safe it is. When he leaves, I start to panic more. My heart pounds in my chest and my eyes are wide in panic.

A hand suddenly brushes against mine and I snap my head to stare at Max. He gives me a reassuring smile, his eyes lighting up. I close my eyes and take a deep breath. I'm going to be fine. Max is with me--that's all that matters. The corners of my lips quirk upwards at the thought.

That's when a voice announces the ride is going to begin.

***

"Oh. My. God." I mumble, stepping off the ride. Max quickly wraps his arm around my shoulder and brings my face into his chest. "You're fine," he whispers into my hair.

I nod my head and hold on tighter to him. That was probably the scariest but fun rides ever. My throat feels a bit sour from all of the screaming but I think it was worth it. At one point during the ride, I was laughing my head off.

"Thank you for that," I tell Max, sincerely.

Max shrugs his shoulders, "you're welcome sunshine. Do you want to find the others now?"

I nod my head and step out of his hold, grabbing his hand. Together, we search for our friends, who could literally be anywhere. This place is so busy, with crowds and crowds of people.

"Do you see them?" I ask Max, standing on my tippy-toes to see above people's heads. "Ugh, why did we think it would be a good idea to split up?"

Max stops walking and stares ahead. I stop too and turn to face him with a frown on my face. "What? Did you find them?" He shakes his head.

"I found someone better."

With my eyebrows still knitted together, I follow his line of sight and gasp at the sight in front of me. Ahead of us, taking photos is Ariana Grande. The celebrity. I absolutely love her, she has an amazing voice. The voice of an angel. Her new album is amazing. The biggest smile I can muster forms on my face. It would be the best thing ever if I could meet her.

"Wanna try and meet her?" Max whispers in my ear. I can just about hear him over the loud chatter and excited screams of fans. I nod my head furiously and drag him over to her, internally squealing.

"Get your phone out," I order when I notice people taking selfies with her. Max complies, not wanting to face my wrath right at this moment.

Pushing through the people, I end up standing right in front of her. She's tall, not as tall as me but close. She smiles when she sees me, causing my brain to go mental.

"Do you want a picture?" She asks me in her soft, sweet voice.

"Y--Yes," I stutter, nervously. Man, meeting a famous celebrity you admire can be tough. I'm super nervous. "Max, can you take a picture of us?" I ask him, keeping my eyes on Ariana.

"Sure," he answers. Ariana and I position ourselves. She wraps an arm around my shoulder and smiles.

"He really likes you," I hear her say through the chatter. I turn to face her, puzzled. "He has stars in his eyes when he looks at you. You're one lucky girl."

More to myself then her, I mumble back: "I know."

After I've got a few photos with her, we part. Me more reluctantly. Max encases his hand with mine and leads us out of the crowd and into a small cafe.

"That was amazing," I breathe. "I can't believe I just met Ariana Grande. She is legitimately one of the best singers ever and I met her! Oh my gosh, I'm hyperventilating."

"Woah, woah," Max says, grabbing my hand over the table. He rubs soothing circles on my hand, whilst giving me a concerned look. "You okay there sunshine?"

"Sure," I gulp in air. "This is going down in my diary as one of the best days of my life. No joke."

"You keep a diary?" Max asks, smirking. "Can I look at what you've written about me?"

"Hey," I protest, "I don't have a diary and even if I did, I wouldn't share it with you." If I did keep a diary, most of it would be filled with stuff about Max. I honestly think it would be embarrassing. Max would tease me for ages about it.

"Are you sure about that sunshine?" Positive.

We continue to talk for about twenty minutes, until the group comes hurtling into the cafe, wearing big smiles. Apparently, Max contacted them when I was with Ariana. I was completely entranced by her I didn't notice him texting them.

Anyways, they said they were close to getting on a ride so afterward they would come and find us. Since it was around lunchtime, we decided to eat at the cafe. I told them all about the death trap I went on and when I met Ariana. Molly insisted I post the image on social media and see how many likes I get.

"Right well, should we head over to the hotel?" Josh suggests later in the day when the park is beginning to shut down.

"I'm beat so that's a yes from me," Lawrence comments, yawning loudly. Soon, Bree ends up yawning and so the yawning loop begins. I snuggle my face in Max's chest, hoping to avoid joining the loop. Max chuckles and tightens his hold on my waist.

We all head back to the hotel that's in the park, tiredly. We booked rooms for two to share. Obviously, Harry and Bree were made to be in the same room together like Max and I. Molly's sharing with Josh, leaving Lawrence and Luke to be in the same room together. That's going to be interesting since Luke claims a girl is going to be visiting his room tonight. If it is true, I don't know what Lawrence will do. Possibly scare her away?

"Come on Sunshine, let's go and cuddle," Max says, loud enough for Molly to hear. She wiggles her eyebrows and watches Max lead me into our room. My cheeks heat up in embarrassment. She is so going to quiz me on what happened tomorrow. Oh god.

"Max," I slap his chest lightly. "You are a menace."

Max smirks, "only for you."

As cheesy as that line is, I still love it. Just because it came from Max.

I roll my eyes, hiding the smile on my face and head into the en-suite bathroom to get changed. After brushing my teeth and hair, I step out and crash onto the bed. Max has already changed into a pair of PJ bottoms, leaving his chest bare. My eyes trail along his tanned skin and six-pack with lust. Despite the fact I've seen his chest a lot, I still stare at it like I've never seen it before.

Max is one hell of an attractive man. I am so lucky to be blessed with him. And it's not just about his looks.

I climb to the end of the bed and cuddle up against Max. He wraps an arm around my shoulder and gestures for me to put my head on his chest. Without a thought, I comply. This feels nice.

No, it feels perfect.

"I love you, Max," I whisper, dazed.

"And I will always love you, Ava." He replies, huskily. "So much."

And that's when my eyes flutter closed, a content smile planted on my face. How I could even think to give this up is beyond me. This right here is heaven.

"I guess I found you." I hear Max say into the darkness. "I found Ava."

The end.

CPSIA information can be obtained
at www.ICGtesting.com
Printed in the USA
LVHW042309071122
732584LV00013B/471